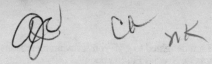

"Lucas, I've had a change of heart. I can't marry you after all."

"The facts haven't changed, Allie. I still need a wife so that I can adopt a child, and you still need money."

"I intend to explore other avenues for the loan." What those would be she had no idea. "I'm sorry I can't help you with your…situation, but marriage is out of the question."

Resting his arms on his desk, he leaned toward her. "Why?"

Why? she asked herself. Why couldn't she marry him? Last night at two a.m., her bedsheets tangled around her legs from her restlessness, she'd had the answers. Now it seemed none of them would hold up to his scrutiny.

"Because we hardly know one another." She groped for the words. "Because marriage…" *Because marriage is far too intimate a relationship. Because it would force a false closeness on us neither one wants.*

Because you kissed me.

D1413314

Dear Reader,

This August, I am delighted to give you six winning reasons to pick up a Silhouette Special Edition book.

For starters, Lindsay McKenna, whose action-packed and emotionally gritty romances have entertained readers for years, moves us with her exciting cross-line series MORGAN'S MERCENARIES: ULTIMATE RESCUE. The first book, *The Heart Beneath,* tells of love against unimaginable odds. With a background as a firefighter in the late 1980s, Lindsay elaborates, "This story is about love, even when buried beneath the rubble of a hotel, or deep within a human being who has been terribly wounded by others, that it will not only survive, but emerge and be victorious."

No stranger to dynamic storytelling, Laurie Paige kicks off a new MONTANA MAVERICKS spin-off with *Her Montana Man,* in which a beautiful forensics examiner must gather evidence in a murder case, but also has to face the town's mayor, a man she'd loved and lost years ago. Don't miss the second book in THE COLTON'S: COMANCHE BLOOD series—Jackie Merritt's *The Coyote's Cry,* a stunning tale of forbidden love between a Native American sheriff and the town's "golden girl."

Christine Rimmer delivers the first romance in her captivating new miniseries THE SONS OF CAITLIN BRAVO. In *His Executive Sweetheart,* a secretary pines for a Bravo bachelor who just happens to be her boss! And in Lucy Gordon's *Princess Dottie,* a waitress-turned-princess is a dashing prince's only chance at keeping his kingdom—and finding true love.... Debut author Karen Sandler warms readers with *The Boss's Baby Bargain,* in which a controlling CEO strikes a marriage bargain with his financially strapped assistant, but their smoldering attraction leads to an unexpected pregnancy!

This month's selections are stellar romances that will put a smile on your face and a song in your heart! Happy reading.

Sincerely,

Karen Taylor Richman
Senior Editor

Please address questions and book requests to:
Silhouette Reader Service
U.S.: 3010 Walden Ave., P.O. Box 1325, Buffalo, NY 14269
Canadian: P.O. Box 609, Fort Erie, Ont. L2A 5X3

The Boss's Baby Bargain

KAREN SANDLER

SPECIAL EDITION™

Published by Silhouette Books

America's Publisher of Contemporary Romance

This one's for the Barbaras: Barbara McMahon,
my mentor and good friend; Barbara Stier, my stepmom
and biggest fan; and Barbara Williams, my mom,
who no doubt keeps them hopping up in heaven.

And special thanks to Jo Cain-Stiles
for helping me understand Lucas.

 SILHOUETTE BOOKS

ISBN 0-373-24488-6

THE BOSS'S BABY BARGAIN

Copyright © 2002 by Karen Sandler

Visit Silhouette at www.eHarlequin.com

Printed in U.S.A.

KAREN SANDLER

first caught the writing bug at age nine when, as a horse-crazy fourth grader, she wrote a poem about a pony named Tony. Many years of hard work later, she sold her first book (and she got that pony—although his name is Ben). She enjoys writing novels, short stories and screenplays and recently produced her first short film. She lives in Northern California with her husband of twenty years and two teenage boys who are busy eating her out of house and home.

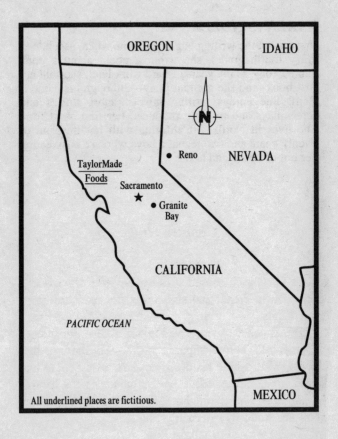

OREGON

IDAHO

N

● Reno

NEVADA

TaylorMade
Foods

Sacramento

★

● Granite
Bay

CALIFORNIA

PACIFIC OCEAN

MEXICO

All underlined places are fictitious.

Chapter One

Allie Dickenson paused at Lucas Taylor's office door, gulping in a breath and smoothing her hair with nervous hands.

She knocked twice, waiting for his impatient, "Come in!" before slipping inside and shutting the door. He sat behind his desk, his dark head bent to his work, his complete focus on the papers in his hands. Breath held, spine straight, she moved to stand before him, her stomach a mass of knots.

"Lucas, I need to talk to you."

He took another moment to finish scribbling a note, then looked up at her, his gray eyes narrowing. Behind him, the morning sun streaming through the window backlit his large frame, casting his face into shadow. "Talk to me? About what?"

She slid her hands into the side pockets of her full

skirt, her fingers clenching into fists. ''Some-thing…somewhat…personal.''

He just stared, still as a tiger stalking prey. She wished he'd look away…back to the papers cluttering his desk, out the floor-to-ceiling window that formed the back wall of his office. But of course he didn't, and Allie had no choice but to meet his hard gaze.

''Personal?'' He raised one brow. ''As in unrelated to your job?''

''Yes…'' The word came out as a near whisper. She swallowed, took another long breath. ''…and no.''

As he fixed his gaze on her, the deep well of wishful thinking inside her imagined something in his eyes, something that set her heart to beating faster. Then his mouth tightened with annoyance. ''I'm busy, Allie. Can you get to the point?''

The knots in Allie's stomach froze into a sickening weight. She forced herself to loosen her fingers, or-dered her shoulders to relax. Forming the words in her mind, she imagined them marching off her tongue. *I need to borrow twenty thousand dollars.* But they wouldn't quite come. ''This is hard for me to say.''

He waited for her to continue, fingers drumming. Then he picked up a pen, stroked its length with his fingertips. Forbidden thoughts arose in her mind as she followed his unconscious gesture. The brief panoply of images that emerged before she could banish them re-minded her of all the reasons asking Lucas for a loan was a bad idea, no matter how desperate she was.

''Is this about your last raise?'' he prodded. ''You don't think I'm paying you enough?''

She shook her head. ''No, no, it's not that.''

If anything, he overpaid. Since she'd joined TaylorMade Foods two years ago, she'd worked hard and had taken on increasing responsibility. But her last employee review had overwhelmed her with its glowing accolades. And the amount of her raise left her gasping. Once the problems with her father had started, though, she was glad for every penny.

"I'm probably the best paid administrative assistant in Sacramento County." She mustered a smile and his gaze sharpened on her in a way that sent heat curling inside her. In spite of herself, she looked away briefly, then back at him. "But I've had some problems recently."

Her hands had scrunched back into fists and she pressed them against her thighs. Despite the fullness of her muted floral-print skirt, he detected the motion, his gaze flicking down to her hips, then dragging back up to her face. There was a message in his gray eyes, in the sharp line of his jaw, one that reached inside her, teased her to translate it— That he was her superior, that he was fourteen years older than her twenty-six years, shrank to insignificance in the face of that enticing lure.

A stunning thought flashed into her mind. Maybe these ridiculous feelings weren't one-sided. Maybe Lucas felt the same way. Maybe—

When he spoke, it took her a moment to understand the quiet words. "Allie, are you in trouble?"

She flushed, all at once mortified and relieved. Thank God he couldn't read her mind. "No," she assured him. "It isn't that at all. It's just—"

His phone jangled on his desk, forwarded from her own phone when she hadn't been there to answer it. She took a step toward his desk, reflexively reaching for the receiver.

Lucas put up a hand to stop her. "I'll get it." He

punched the lighted button on the phone console and lifted the receiver. "Lucas Taylor."

He listened a moment, then glanced up at her. "I'll have to get back to you, John. Give me two minutes." Hanging up the phone, he said to Allie, "Can we finish our conversation later?"

Even as she felt relief at the reprieve, she worried that waiting would only make the words harder to say. She nodded. "Let me know when you have time."

"You know my schedule better than I do. When do I have time?"

She squelched her irritation at his abrupt tone. She thought she'd learned not to react to his arrogance. It must be her unease about their conversation that had her off-balance. "You have an hour after lunch."

"Come back then." His gaze lowered to his papers. When she didn't turn immediately, he looked up again. "Anything else?"

She shook her head. "No, nothing." She quickly turned on her heel and let herself out of his office, shutting the door behind her.

Crossing to her desk with two long strides, she sank into her chair. Her hands covering her face, she wondered which was the biggest mess—her father's crisis or the impossible situation with her boss.

What had started as a dimly remembered erotic dream had quickly flowered into a series of daytime fantasies that she couldn't seem to stop. She'd allowed herself the indulgence at first because the fantasies distracted her from her loneliness, never mind the inappropriateness of the central figure. But her daydreams had recently taken on a life of their own, until the sexual images had drifted into decidedly unwanted emotions. Feelings for a man she truly didn't know.

She dropped her hands from her face and glanced back at the door to Lucas's office. Considering the craziness of her feelings for him, she'd nearly talked herself out of asking him for the loan. But where else could she go? She didn't have an asset to her name worth borrowing against. Her brother and sister were both struggling to support their own families. If they knew their father's money was all gone, they would help her in a heartbeat. But they didn't know, and she planned to keep it that way.

Agitated, she tugged open her bottom desk drawer and pulled out a plastic bag of bread scraps. She needed to get out of the office, needed a break from the emotions churning inside her. Some time outside would give her a chance to regain a bit of calm.

Setting her phone to ring through to Lucas's office, she hurried to the elevators and escape.

Lucas stared down at his telephone, his finger hovering above the keypad. The urgency of his business with his attorney, John Evans, had faded into the background the moment Allie had appeared in his office. What had once been an obsession had been bumped to second place just by her presence. Hell, he had completely forgotten he'd asked John to call him this morning.

All because of Allie. Allie, who had become invaluable to him in the last two years. Allie, who had singlehandedly brought order to his hectic schedule and the extensive travel his work demanded.

Allie, who in the last several months had intruded on nearly every waking thought, weaving her way into his every sensual fantasy.

He knew it wasn't right. He knew he was one inadvertent touch away from sexual harassment. Yet sometimes it was all he could do to keep himself from reaching out to test the softness of her hair, the smoothness of her cheek.

Shoving back his chair, he rose to his feet and turned to gaze out the window. Five stories below, the campus of TaylorMade Foods stretched out before him. Despite the late-summer heat of the Sacramento Valley, the rolling hills between the buildings of TaylorMade's headquarters glowed a verdant green. Trees dotted the landscape—valley oak and scrub pine. At the center of the three five-story structures, like the hub of a three-spoke wheel, a pond glimmered in the midmorning sunlight.

The king of all I survey, Lucas thought darkly.

As he watched, a solitary swan skimmed across the surface of the pond. It was all his—the pond, the swan and its mate hiding somewhere in the reeds, the buildings of wood and stone and glass, the TaylorMade corporation. He'd worked hard for all of it, yet the sight of all that neatly landscaped beauty filled him with an edgy dissatisfaction.

Feeling a heaviness inside him, he turned back to the phone and stabbed out his attorney's number. When John answered, Lucas didn't waste time with preliminaries. "Sorry. What did you find out?"

John had known him too long to be put off by his brusqueness. "The county adoption agency said no way. They won't even look at your application."

He'd expected as much, but still the news twisted his insides. He fixed his gaze on the swan below, watching its passage. He wished he had a tenth of the serenity of the graceful white bird. "What about private adoption agencies?"

His attorney let out a sigh before he answered. "It'll be the same story there."

As the swan's mate emerged from the thick cluster of reeds at the pond's edge, Lucas caught sight of someone striding across the lawn toward the water. Allie. "Are you telling me it's impossible?"

"I told you at the outset this wouldn't be easy. The agencies give top priority to married couples."

As if she were right beside him instead of a hundred yards away on the lawn below, Lucas felt heat spreading in his loins. With an effort, he returned his attention to the conversation with his attorney. "I doubt many parents could give a child what I can."

John hesitated, as if choosing his words carefully. "Materially, no."

Lucas heard the unspoken message, the one the usually straightforward John had danced around since Lucas had first announced his intention to adopt. With his wealth, Lucas could give a child anything he or she might desire. As for what the child might need...

He watched Allie reach into the plastic bag she'd brought with her and toss something out onto the pond toward the swans. The grace of her every movement drew him, set off an ache inside. "What about that attorney friend of yours?"

"The teenage girl he represents already found placement for her baby with a young couple."

The swans approached the grassy shore in tandem, gobbling up the treats as they swam. Allie reached precariously out over the water to drop more bread scraps for the birds, then straightened to empty the last of the bag. Lucas took too much damn pleasure in watching her movements, as lithe as the swans she fed.

He turned resolutely away from the window. "You

said he came in contact with a number of unwed teen-age mothers.''

"He does," John said slowly. "Look, I know I've mentioned this before and you've dismissed it out-right—"

"No," Lucas said, knowing where John was leading.

He continued doggedly, ''—but you really ought to consider a more conventional—"

"No."

"Just because your marriage with Carol didn't work out—"

"No. I won't marry."

There was a long silence as John seemed to digest his flat refusal. "Then forget about adopting. You're forty years old—"

"Is it a matter of money?" He couldn't help himself; he turned back to the window. But Allie had gone, no doubt back into the building. The swans drifted to-gether across the pond. "If greasing the wheels would speed the process—"

"There aren't any wheels to grease. Hell, you can't buy a child."

Self-recrimination settled inside him, sharp and bit-ter. This was exactly what he had feared. That despite good intentions, what was most crucial for a child was beyond his capacity to provide. "John, I've got to go. Get back to that attorney friend and get another refer-ral."

"If you'll think about my suggestion."

He wouldn't, but no point in telling John that. "Call me later in the week."

Slipping the phone back into its cradle, he tugged open the middle desk drawer to retrieve the bottle of antacids. He tossed three into his mouth and chewed the tart, chalky tablets with a grimace. He'd been downing far too many of the antacids, a point his doctor had made at his last checkup a couple months ago. His doctor had told him to relax, to slow down, as if that would cure what was eating away at him inside.

Women and their damn biological clocks didn't have anything on his own urgency for a child. Everything he'd worked for for the last twenty years, every goal had narrowed down to a single purpose—to provide for his progeny. He had amassed a fortune, more money than a man could spend in his lifetime, and everything in him insisted he pass it on to someone. No brothers or sisters, no parents—a knot twisted inside him painfully—he had to give what he possessed to a child, a child of his own.

He didn't completely understand his own motives. As a boy, he'd dreamed of wealth and riches. He'd longed for something as simple as a home of his own during the long, lonely nights spent in a strange bed at yet another foster placement. If he could save even one boy or girl from a life like his, it might begin to make up for those years of deprivation.

Or at least that was what he told himself.

He never would have let Carol go if he'd felt the urgency for a son or daughter so strongly seven years ago. He would have found a way to keep her. Never mind that there was no love lost between them, he would have tied her down somehow. Hell, he might have even made her pregnant, if he could have been sure the child would inherit her genes and not his. It was just as well he'd felt differently then. To have brought a child into a marriage like his and Carol's would have been cruel.

He pressed his palm against the wall of glass behind his desk, gazed down on his domain. The swan and her mate had disappeared back into the reeds. The breathless stillness of late summer left the man-made pond surface mirror-smooth, forming a near-perfect oval. That was his life, a construction of perfection, from the neatly manicured lawns of the TaylorMade campus to the sleek barren lines of his home in nearby Granite Bay. From the artwork lining the walls of his home to the acres of tastefully decorated office space, he lived a perfect life.

If only his soul weren't so damned empty.

Shooting the cuffs of his jacket, he checked the time on the slim gold watch on his wrist. He had a meeting scheduled in ten minutes with research and development in one of the other buildings. Then there was a lunchtime interview for a project lead position opening up soon. Then, finally, he could return to his office and resume his conversation with Allie.

Although talk was the last thing he wanted to do with her. He wanted her in his arms, pressed against his body. He wanted to bury his face in the silk of her hair, to grab a handful of her soft skirt and ease it up her legs. To inhale her beguiling scent and trail his tongue down the slender column of her throat.

Good God, what the hell was he thinking? Gritting his teeth against his body's response to the all-too-vivid images, he slammed his chair into the well of his desk. Gathering up the papers scattered across the desk, he stuffed them into his briefcase and headed for the door.

Allie wasn't at her desk—thank God for that. Lord only knew what he might do with the tantalizing images still dancing in his head. Stepping past her desk, he headed for the elevators and slapped the down button.

When the elevator door opened, he wasn't prepared for the sight of Allie inside, head bent down, arms crossed over her middle. When her head swung up and she met his gaze, the impact of the visual contact felt as physical as a punch to the gut. The eager fantasies started up again, made more real by her presence. His hungry gaze took in the picture she made—her wary green eyes, the silky dark hair brushing her shoulders, the contrast of her pale arms to the copper-colored shell top she wore. Her flowered skirt reached nearly to her ankles, but somehow it was more provocative than the shortest of minis.

The door started to close; he reached out a hand to stop it. Her gaze fell from his as color rose in her cheeks. She moved past him out of the elevator. "Sorry," she said, her low voice setting off new flares inside him.

He stepped inside the elevator, keeping a hand on the door. "I'll be over in R and D."

She seemed to want to look anywhere but at him. Good God, had she somehow picked up on his ridiculous middle-aged fantasies? That would be a disaster. At the least she'd want to transfer into another department. At the worst she might leave TaylorMade entirely, take a position at another firm.

The elevator buzzed, cutting into his thoughts. He wished she'd look up at him, so he could try to read what might be on her mind. The elevator buzzed again, so he called out, "See you after lunch," then let go of the door. Just before it shut, she did look up at him, but damned if he could interpret what he'd seen in that brief glimpse of her green gaze.

As he rode the elevator down, his stomach roiled with an unfamiliar anxiety. The sudden fear that Allie might leave, that his own lack of control might have driven her away dug its claws into him. When he should have been planning for the meeting ahead of him, his mind wouldn't leave that fear alone.

Was that what she'd come to talk to him about this morning? That she planned to leave the company? Despite his every effort to keep his feelings hidden, had she somehow sensed his passion for her? Lord, no wonder she'd seemed so skittish. She was probably afraid he'd make a play for her at any moment.

He was such a damned idiot. Striding through the downstairs lobby, he gave the glass door leading to the outside a savage push. As he followed the concrete pathway leading to the next building, he ran over and over every nuance of what Allie had said—and hadn't said—this morning.

As he did, snatches of his conversation with John interwove themselves in his mind with images of Allie, and a preposterous idea floated briefly into his consciousness. He didn't allow himself even a moment's consideration before abandoning the notion. Instead he concentrated on the points he would use to counter Allie's intent to leave.

He'd convince her that her impressions were wrong. That what she'd sensed from him had been merely his admiration for her abilities as his admin assistant. Because that was all that really mattered—her value to him as an employee. The rest was just his ill-timed lack of control, a weakness of approaching middle age.

Tugging open the door to the research and development building, he forced his attention back to his scheduled meeting. For the next hour he kept his focus there, his mind straying to thoughts of Allie no more than a half dozen times during the meeting.

When Allie returned to her desk after lunch, she found a yellow sticky note on her phone. She recognized the handwriting on it immediately as Lucas's hasty scrawl.

Problem in R and D.
Have to postpone our meeting.

—L.

She stared at the brief message with Lucas's extravagant looping *L* at the bottom. He'd taken the time to write her a note? Ordinarily he'd bark out a few words to whoever was nearby, leaving Allie to ask around to discover his whereabouts.

She was even more surprised when he called twenty minutes later, launching into his explanation without even a hello. ''The developers and marketing are at each other's throat. This might take the rest of the day.''

Even the sound of his voice set off a trembling inside her. Eyes shut, she held the phone to her ear and willed herself to be calm. ''No rush,'' she said, even though her father's dilemma pressed in on her. ''We can try again tomorrow.''

He paused, piquing her curiosity further. ''What about dinner? Are you free?''

''Dinner? Tonight?'' She had nothing planned, but dinner with Lucas seemed terribly...intimate. Part of her ached to say yes even as her mind warned that she would be treading into dangerous territory.

''If you have a date...''

"No," Allie said quickly. "Dinner tonight would be fine. What time?"

"Six? Gives me a deadline for this group."

A deadline. Of course. Dinner with her gave him an excuse to call an end to what would likely be an interminable meeting. There was nothing intimate about it.

"Six is fine. I'll meet you in the lobby." She pulled his calendar toward her, determined to be businesslike. "What about your afternoon appointments?"

"What have I got?"

"Two meetings, another interview." She read the details from the calendar.

"Attend the meetings in my place. Get Randy Sato to do the interview. Got to go."

"See you—" But he hung up before she could get the words out.

Allie sagged back in her chair, trying to quiet the clamor inside her. This couldn't go on much longer, her feeling this way and working so closely with Lucas. She had to get over her silly schoolgirl crush. Before long, someone would notice. At the least, it would be terribly embarrassing. At the worst, she might well lose her job.

She didn't even want to think about that possibility, not with the situation with her father so dire. She had to keep a level head, for her father's sake.

Turning to her computer, she printed off the documents she needed for the two afternoon meetings, then caught up on some correspondence. When the time for the first meeting rolled around, she had her focus back, her mind on work. Yes, she had to return to her desk twice before she'd even reached the elevator—once to get her laptop, once to retrieve the papers she'd care-

fully printed for the meetings. And she did draw a
blank on the names of two of the attendees—people
she'd known for the entire two years she'd worked at
TaylorMade. But her dinner with Lucas didn't intrude
on her thoughts at all.

Not much, anyway.

His fingers wrapped around the steering wheel of his
Mercedes, Lucas glanced again at the rearview mirror.
Allie was still behind him in her ten-year-old Buick,
her face barely visible through the sun-gilded windshield. When he'd first seen her rattletrap car, he'd
nearly insisted she ride with him in the Benz, just to
be certain she'd make it to the restaurant. But the Buick
had started right up, its badly tuned engine rattling and
knocking as it idled.

The Mercedes's engine purred as he took the turn
onto Auburn-Folsom Road toward the American River.
As Allie's car lagged behind him, barely making the
light, Lucas mentally included "company car" on the
list of inducements he planned to present to her tonight.
Added to the package he'd already put together, she
couldn't possibly say no.

Nevertheless, anxiety dug away at his gut. He
shouldn't have taken that damn call from his attorney
just before he left the office. It was only more bad news
and it had thrown him off his stride, set him to second-
guessing his strategy for handling Allie. The two had
nothing to do with each other, no connection whatso-
ever. His failure to adopt had no bearing on his ability
to retain the best admin assistant TaylorMade had ever
hired.

Turning into the Cliff House Restaurant parking lot,
he maneuvered his silver sedan into a space, then

quickly crossed to Allie's car to open her door. She looked up at him, her startled green eyes a tantalizing enticement. Reaching across for her purse, she laid her fingers in his outstretched palm and rose from the car. She quickly pulled her hand free, turning to shut the car door.

Keep your damn hands off her, Taylor! He followed her into the Cliff House, maintaining a good two feet of space between them. When he stepped around her to open the restaurant door for her, he made certain he didn't rest a hand at the small of her back or brush his fingers along her arm. But his mind went wild imagining it.

It was still fairly early and the restaurant was half empty. The maître d' led them to a window table overlooking the American River. The setting sun glittered on the broad swath of water below, a nearly blinding display.

Lucas waited until the maître d' had finished fussing with menus and water glasses before he launched into his campaign. "Before you say anything, I want you to know I can match any salary."

"What?" Her eyes widened, momentarily distracting him.

He pushed on. "And I can accelerate your vesting. Four years instead of five."

Her brow furrowed. "Lucas, what are you talking about?"

"I don't intend to let you leave the company."

"What? Oh!" She smiled, and his body reacted immediately to that simple curving of her lips. "I'm sorry."

Thinking she was apologizing because she'd already made up her mind, he opened his mouth to offer another of the persuasions he'd devised. But then she reached across the table to lay her hand over the back of his and his good sense fragmented in that light touch.

His teeth clenched, his jaw worked to keep himself from turning his hand on the table to clasp her fingers in his. He dug his fingertips into the white linen tablecloth until he thought he would tear holes in the sturdy fabric. His eyes on her small hand, he felt her warmth melting into his skin.

He glanced up at her, her gaze tangling with his. One moment they seemed joined by an intangible but unbreakable cord, the next she was snatching her hand away, color rising in her face. Lucas forced himself to leave his hand where it was, ignoring the chill that seemed to brush against it now that her touch was gone.

She dropped her hands to her lap, and her gaze fell to the white linen. "I'm not leaving the company, Lucas." She tipped her chin up. "I need a loan."

He tried to understand what she was saying. "A loan?"

She bobbed her head. "From you, Lucas. Twenty thousand dollars." Her voice faltered slightly over the amount.

She wasn't leaving! A weight seemed to lift inside him at the news. Yet his relief made him feel somehow vulnerable. He hardened that softness inside him. "Why?"

At first he thought she wouldn't answer. "It's personal. I'd rather leave it at that."

Her evasiveness made him feel justified in being harsh with her. "You expect me to give you twenty thousand dollars—"

Her eyes burned with green fire. "Not give…loan."

"—*loan* you twenty thousand without any reason?"

To her credit, she kept her gaze on him. "I'm not in trouble, Lucas. This isn't to pay off a gambling debt run up in Tahoe or a stack of credit-card bills. But it is personal. I'd hoped that in the two years I've worked for you I'd proved myself—"

"Yes."

Her mouth hung open a moment as she absorbed what he'd said. "Yes? You'll loan me the money?"

He gave her a clipped nod, the enormity of what was falling into place inside him nearly making him shake all over. *It's a business decision, nothing more,* he told himself, but still it took a good long breath for him to continue.

"I'll give you the money," he said. "On one condition."

She swallowed, the motion of her throat begging him to touch her there. "What condition?"

"Marry me."

Chapter Two

Allie couldn't possibly have heard him right. She stared at his implacable face, waiting for him to continue, to clarify what he'd said. But he just stared back at her, his gray eyes unfathomable.

"Marry?" She swallowed, shaking her head. "You?"

For an instant, he seemed flustered, then he gathered his usual cloak of arrogance around him. "Hear me out."

He leaned back in his chair, his gaze falling a moment to the linen tablecloth. She knew that impenetrable expression, had seen it dozens of time during staff meetings or when he was in the midst of acquisition negotiations. It meant he felt fully in control of the proceedings and intended to turn circumstances exactly the way he desired.

"Lucas—" she began, but he forestalled her with a raised hand.

"Hear me out," he said again.

He lowered his hands to the edge of the table, his fingers gripping so tightly, his knuckles whitened. Allie suddenly realized he wasn't nearly as in control as she'd thought.

He kept his eyes fixed on her as if it were an effort of will. "For the past several months, I've been attempting to adopt."

"A baby?" she asked, incredulous.

"Or a young child." He cleared his throat. "The county doesn't want to approve a forty-year-old single man. My attorney tells me I could even the odds considerably if I married."

He made the process sound so cut-and-dried, she might have thought he considered a child one more step in the well-thought-out business plan of his life. Yet she detected the faintest tremor in his voice, a shadow of desperation in his eyes. This from a man who remained aloof when employees brought their children into the office.

"Lucas, we hardly know one another. To marry—"

"If it's sex you're worried about..."

Sex! Good God, she hadn't even considered the physical side of a marriage to Lucas. Despite herself, her mind raced, her heart rate keeping pace. All the fantasies she'd struggled to contain surged forward.

"...I'm not proposing a conventional marriage," Lucas continued, oblivious to her rampant thoughts. "It would be strictly platonic."

The sudden rush of disappointment unsettled her. Pushing it aside, she focused on rational discussion.

"Why me? There must be other women, women you've dated who could play the role of wife."

"They have much more complex lives than you. They've been married before, have children, their own homes. You have no strings."

True enough, but she felt irritation at the dismissive way he summed up her life. Allie shook her head. "Strings or not, I'm not interested in marriage."

"Look," Lucas said, reaching across the table to take her hand. She couldn't suppress a shiver of reaction. "I need a wife, you need money. Agree to marry me and we both get what we want."

His large hand covered hers, his warm palm nestling against her fingers. The warmth, the power of him seemed to sap her strength, to dissolve her will. Like her autocratic father, this man could swallow her up, diminish her.

Her own mother, a sweet and loving woman, had always seemed to shrink in stature when she was with her husband. French Dickenson barked out an order and Elizabeth complied, even if it turned her own plans upside down. Allie's mother gave every ounce of her soul to the man she adored, tucking her own needs away time and again. When the cancer took hold, Elizabeth's physical pain was nothing compared to the agony she had felt in defying French by dying.

Allie was not her mother. She couldn't live like that. "No." She tugged her hand free. "I can't marry you."

His jaw tightened and she recognized the hard light in his gray eyes. "Then I can't loan you the money."

Allie sat there, stunned. Not that he would turn her down, but that he would coerce her this way. To back her into a corner went beyond arrogance, bordered on cruelty.

"You can't mean that."

"I can. It's my money, Allie."

She looked around her at the half-full restaurant, at the waiter hovering nearby, out the window at the American River below them. She couldn't say yes, couldn't let herself be sucked into Lucas's control. She faced him again. "Then I'll get the money somewhere else."

A faint smile curved his lips. "If you could have borrowed it elsewhere, you wouldn't have asked me. I'm your last resort."

Of course he was right, damn him. And he surely knew how desperately she needed the money. Still, the words were impossible to drag out. "If I agreed, how long would we have to stay married?"

The tension in his face eased at her apparent capitulation. "One year, possibly two. However long it takes to finalize the adoption. I'll have to consult my attorney."

She nodded, her head suddenly pounding. She felt as if she perched on the lip of a chasm, readying herself to leap it. Would she safely reach the other side? Or fall to be crushed on the rocks below? "Then yes," she said, barely above a whisper. "I'll marry you."

Triumph lit his eyes—triumph and something else. Relief? "Good then. Fine." He picked up his water glass to sip; she could swear his hand trembled slightly. "A month enough time for you? To pack up your apartment and move to my estate?"

The enormity of what she'd agreed to swamped her. "Move? Why can't I keep my own place?"

"Social services performs home visitations for prospective parents. They'll expect husband and wife to be living together.''

She imagined herself standing in the river below, the swift currents below the surface taking her feet out from under her, sweeping her away. She tried to grasp for some measure of self-control. "When can you give me the money?"

He gestured peremptorily to the waiter. "After we're married.''

"No," she said, grateful for the opportunity to take a stand, no matter how weak. "I need the money now.''

"That's acceptable." He opened the menu, effectively dismissing her now that he had her concession. "I'll wire the money to your account tomorrow."

He ordered for them both, scarcely pausing to ask her approval of his choice. Shaken by what had transpired in the past several minutes, she realized she would have to strengthen her resolve if she hoped to survive this…this…agreement with Lucas with her self-esteem intact.

When her salad arrived, she dove into it, suddenly ravenous. She'd been so anxious about her upcoming discussion with Lucas, she'd eaten almost nothing at lunch. Now, with a little food in her stomach, she could wrest some control back from Lucas.

"Where shall we have the ceremony?" she asked.

He seemed surprised by her question. "The county courthouse. Or Tahoe. It doesn't matter."

She tipped her chin up stubbornly. "It does to me. I want my family there. They'd never forgive me if I didn't invite them."

"It isn't a real wedding, **Allie**. We don't need your family there."

He was right, of course. There was no real commitment between them other than expediency. But she felt a compulsion to include her family. "I need them."

"No." He shook his head. "I don't want this turning into a circus."

"Not a circus, Lucas. Just my sister, brother and their spouses."

His gaze narrowed on her and she got the sense he was only now realizing he may have underestimated her. She felt a brief flare of satisfaction. Then he dipped his head in acquiescence. "Fine. We'll include your family."

She ought to be content with that victory, but she pushed on. "And I want the ceremony in a church, not the courthouse."

She expected exasperation. Instead she got cold, tightly leashed anger. "Not a church. The courthouse or my own backyard. I won't say the vows in a church."

The bitterness in his tone, the bleak rage in his eyes shocked her. "The courthouse, then," she said softly.

Even as he retreated behind his habitual arrogant mask, Allie wondered about the true self hidden beneath the layers of control, wondered if there was anything more to Lucas Taylor than the overbearing persona he showed the world.

Maybe not. Maybe some men, like Lucas, like her own father, only knew one way—power, control, dominance. Give and take, compromise didn't exist in their universe. In all the years and all the battles with her father, Allie would have given anything for a truce. But in her father's eyes, truce meant surrender and surrender meant defeat.

In the end, his own body had defeated him. As his

lucent moments became scarcer, her father might never realize the way his daughter had sacrificed her own freedom on his behalf.

Leaning back as the waiter came to take away their salad plates, Allie felt the significance of her agreement with Lucas settle on her, a nearly unbearable weight. The delectable broiled salmon the waiter set before her a few moments later could have been sawdust for all the appeal it held for her roiling stomach. As she made a show of cutting a bite of the succulent fish, she glanced over at Lucas.

He sat motionless, looking out the window, his expression distant, his face emotionless. While she struggled to come to terms with the prospect of marriage, Lucas seemed to have already compartmentalized it as another finalized business decision. It meant no more to him than that.

Her gaze dropped to the table and saw a different story in Lucas's hands. Resting on either side of his plate of swordfish, they gripped his fork and knife so fiercely she wondered if he would bend them in his agitation. Tension popped the tendons out in the backs of his hands, set his shoulders into a stiff, rigid line.

"Lucas." She reached out, lightly touched his hand.

He jerked back from her, dropping the silverware. "Excuse me." Tossing his napkin on the table, he rose and strode off toward the men's room.

Allie watched him go, a thousand questions whirling in her mind. She ate a few bites of her salmon, a little of the fresh broccoli beside it on the plate, all the while forcing herself to sit still and wait for Lucas.

When he returned, he'd gathered his businesslike shroud around him again. "We can have the ceremony at a church, if you like." He said it as if it mattered little to him, as if his vehement objection earlier had never happened. "I'll leave it to you to pick the church."

He dug into his swordfish then, finishing it off methodically. No explanation of why he'd left the table, no further discussion of the wedding. Allie could scarcely take another bite, he had her so off-balance.

Later, when he escorted her to her car, he opened the door for her and waited until she'd climbed inside. "Last Saturday in September," he said. "The afternoon is fine."

She might as well have been scheduling a business trip for him. "Have you considered what we should tell people at work?"

He shrugged. "They know how closely we've worked together the past two years. We'll announce we've decided to marry. They'll draw their own conclusions."

It might be that easy for him. Most of TaylorMade's employees were too intimidated to ask Lucas any personal questions. But she had a half dozen friends at the office who would grill her mercilessly when they found out.

He gazed down at her, his expression inscrutable. "That's it, then."

She waited for him to back away, to shut the door. Instead, he bent, leaning into the car, brushing his lips against her cheek. Then his hand cupped her chin, turning her toward him. He pressed his lips to hers, softly, his lingering warmth stealing her breath.

She couldn't help herself, she kissed him back, slanting her mouth against his, raising her hand to his rough cheek. She heard a low sound in his throat, felt his fingers on her chin tighten. Then the briefest stroke of his tongue against the seam of her lips easing her mouth open. She parted her lips, ready to welcome him inside.

He straightened abruptly, backing away from her. "Sorry," he rasped out before slamming her door. Rounding his car, he wrenched open his door, every movement full of anger. He waited until she'd started her engine and pulled out, but he wouldn't look her way.

Her entire body shook in the aftermath of his kiss and the anger that followed it. As she navigated the streets back to her apartment, she kept a stranglehold on the steering wheel to keep from veering off the road.

She'd thought she could handle this. She'd thought she could marry Lucas and still keep her sanity. But now she realized it was entirely impossible. His kiss had brought home to her the utter lunacy of the notion.

She'd tell him tomorrow. First thing in the morning, when she walked into his office, she'd tell him she'd changed her mind. She'd just have to scare up another source of money.

Agitated, she missed the turn at Sunrise and had to double back. As she wended her way through the traffic, she tried to rehearse what she would say to Lucas. But despite all her efforts, her mind kept returning to the feel of his lips on hers, the strength of his hand cupping her face.

Lucas shut the front door behind him and tossed his keys on the small table in the spacious entryway. Through sheer will he kept himself from flinging his briefcase across the acres of Berber carpeting his living room. He dropped it under the table, unwilling for the moment to open it and pull out the work he'd brought home.

What the hell had he done? What madness had taken control of him, had driven him to kiss Allie? What had possessed him to suggest marriage in the first place?

He slipped out of his shoes and padded across the glowing oak hardwood of the entryway to the thick living-room carpet. At the far end of the wide room with its high ceilings and expanse of windows over-looking the three-acre lake below stood a fully stocked wet bar. The housekeeper, Mrs. Vasquez, always filled the ice bucket before she left for the day. Lucas pulled down a tumbler and dropped in a handful of ice.

An array of liquor bottles crowded the shelf above. Why did he keep so much alcohol in the house when he never entertained? Some damn test he supposed. To prove he could resist what had destroyed his mother, to refute the potential in his own genetic makeup.

Resolutely, he chose a bottle of tonic water and emp-tied it into the tumbler. A dish of cut lime waited for him in the small refrigerator under the wet bar. After squeezing a wedge into his glass, he moved to the sofa and sagged into it.

He took a swallow of the tart tonic water then set the tumbler aside. It had all seemed so logical in the moment. He needed a wife, she needed money, just as he'd said. But it was apparent from his lack of control when he walked her to his car that it had been his libido talking, not his brain.

He picked up the glass again, glided it back and forth against his brow. What now? There was really only one course of action—tell Allie he'd changed his mind, that after giving the matter consideration, he'd realized a marriage between them would be untenable. He'd loan

her the money as he'd promised and work out an arrangement to deduct payments from her paycheck.

And the solution to his problem—the complete un-
likelihood that the county would relent and decide him
eligible to adopt? He'd have to find another way,
through private agencies or contacts made through his
attorney, John. Those prospects were just as bleak for
a single father and time was certainly against him. But
at least he had the money to pursue that route.

Rising, he walked to the kitchen to check his answering machine. There were two messages, both from
John, both since he'd left his office. Without much
hope, Lucas picked up his portable phone and headed
out the back of the house. This side faced a grove of
oak trees and the small vineyard he'd had put in four
years ago. Leaning against the porch rail, he speed-
dialed his attorney's home number and waited for him
to pick up.

After the greetings were out of the way, John cut to
the chase. "Did I ever introduce you to my cousin,
Angela?"

Lucas pressed his lips into a grim smile. "I don't
want you fixing me up, John."

"But I think you two might hit it off," John persisted. "She's in her early thirties, absolutely gorgeous
and ready to settle down. I told her about you—"

"Not interested, John." Lucas paused, sipped his
drink. "Besides, I've already made my own arrangements."

"What arrangements?"

His hand shaking, Lucas had to set the glass on the
porch rail. His decision of a few moments before might
as well have never been. "I've asked someone to marry me."

Total silence on the phone line. Lucas waited for John to muster a response. After several seconds, his attorney asked, "Who?"

"Allie Dickenson, my admin assistant."

"I had no idea there was anything between you and—"

"There isn't," Lucas said flatly. "I explained the adoption situation to Allie and she agreed to help me out."

"Just like that." John sounded dubious.

"Not entirely. She's in a financial bind. I promised her some money in exchange."

It sounded so crass, laid out like that. He didn't like the negative light Allie's promise to marry him shed on her.

"I see," John said. "And how long will your...commitment last?"

Tension tightened in Lucas's stomach at John's evasion of the word *marriage*. "Until the adoption is finalized. I hope things will move faster with the hurdles out of the way."

"Even with private adoption, that could be a year or two," John cautioned.

"I told her as much." A year or two of living with Allie filled Lucas with an unexpected excitement. He paced across the porch, moving from one end of the house to the other.

John's next statement brought him back to earth. "I assume you'll want a pre-nup drawn up."

A prenuptial agreement? Lucas hadn't even considered that aspect. Something in him balked at the idea of asking Allie to sign a document protecting his assets. It seemed an insult to a woman who had been nothing but honorable as long as he'd known her. "Is that necessary?"

"I highly recommend it," John said.

Lucas sighed. "How soon can you have it ready?"

"When's the wedding?"

"Last weekend in September."

"I'll have it done by the end of next week."

His mind working feverishly, Lucas re-crossed the porch. Beyond him, the gnarled branches of his vineyard glowed orange in the last of the setting sun, each vine heavy with grapes, Chardonnay and Zinfandel. He had so much, surely he could spare more than the twenty thousand he'd promised.

"I want to include a sizeable settlement for Allie." Lucas named an amount, then immediately wondered if he should double it.

"You can't be serious!" John protested. "Carol didn't even get that much."

"There wasn't as much to give back then. Allie's sacrificing one or more years of her life. It's only fair."

A thought niggled at him that it might have been fairest to simply loan her the money without the commitment of marriage. But he pushed it aside, determined to continue.

After he said his goodbyes to John, he considered calling Allie. He wanted to tell her about the pre-nup, about the additional compensation he was awarding her. He felt an urgency to cement the deal between them.

Pushing open the French doors leading back into the house, he strode to the kitchen cabinet where the phone books were kept. He could boot up his computer and get her home number from the company database, but this would be quicker. He'd found her number and was about to dial it when doubt lapped at him. Maybe he should leave her be tonight. He'd already dumped a mountain of turmoil in her lap, maybe she needed some breathing space.

He set down the phone on the counter and headed for the stairs, pausing only to grab his briefcase. But two hours later, he'd accomplished none of the tasks he'd brought home with him. He could think of nothing but Allie's face, her lips, the taste and feel of her against his tongue. Just as he thrust aside one sensual image, another rose to take its place.

It was only lust, he told himself, and lust he could control. As long as those baser feelings didn't give way to other, more intimate, more vulnerable emotions, he would be safe.

So, as he lay in his bed courting sleep, he allowed himself the harmless fantasies. When he finally slept, the eroticism followed him into his dreams. But as morning neared, the sensual haze parted and he saw only Allie's face, her soft green eyes on him, her lips curved in a smile.

When he woke, he refused to acknowledge the inexplicable ache inside him. But it clung to him, nonetheless, as he dressed, ate a hurried breakfast, drove to TaylorMade headquarters. It eased only when he walked off the elevator and saw Allie waiting for him, a tentative smile on her face.

Chapter Three

Everything had changed, Allie realized as she watched Lucas stride toward her desk. Because of their agreement…because of their kiss. Telling him she'd had second thoughts, that she no longer intended to go through with the marriage wouldn't bring things between them back the way they were before. In that one moment when his lips touched hers, the world had shuddered to a stop on its axis and had begun to spin an entirely different way.

He nodded at her as he passed, then waited at his door for her to follow. She wondered if he'd read her mind, had realized she wanted to talk to him. Then she remembered this was the way they started every morning, with his appointment book, going over his day.

As she picked up the laptop computer she stored all his engagements on, she mentally placed her declaration at the top of their to-do list. She had no intention of letting this slide as she had her request for a loan. They had to clear the air immediately.

She shut the door behind her, then crossed the room to set the computer in its usual place on his desk. As it powered up, she opened her mouth to speak.

He beat her to it. "I spoke to my attorney last night and this morning. There are a few details about the marriage we need to go over."

No mention of their kiss, as if it had never happened. Lucas was back in control and Allie realized he could easily steamroller her if she let him.

She stood up straighter before him. "Lucas, I've had a change of heart. I can't marry you after all."

Not a flicker of reaction in his face. He just sat down and motioned her to do the same. "The facts haven't changed, Allie. Your needs and mine dovetail. I've already arranged to have the funds you requested transferred. Just give me your account number."

As she brought the visitor chair up to the desk opposite him, she tried to frame what she'd rehearsed late into the night. She lowered herself into her chair, sat perched on the edge. "I intend to explore other avenues for the loan." What those would be she had no idea. "I'm sorry I can't help you with your...situation, but marriage is out of the question."

Resting his arms on his desk, he leaned toward her. "Why?"

It was barely a question, more a demand for information. Why? she asked herself. Why couldn't she marry him? Last night at 2:00 a.m., her bedsheets tangled around her legs from her restlessness, she'd had the answers. Now it seemed none of them would hold up to his scrutiny.

"Because we hardly know one another." She groped

for the words. "Because marriage..." *Because marriage is far too intimate a relationship. Because it would force a false closeness on us neither one wants.*

Because you kissed me.

"Allie." He said her name so softly, almost tenderly, bringing her attention to him. His steel-gray gaze fixed on her face, his expression intent. "What I did last night...it was a mistake. A ridiculous mistake. I won't repeat it. I promised you a platonic relationship. You have no reason to fear I'll overstep those bounds again."

Under his scrutiny, she could barely bring two thoughts together. "Even still, Lucas—"

"Please reconsider, Allie."

Every ounce of self-preservation within her screamed no. His promise didn't change the thread of attraction stretching between them, her secret yearning that Lucas would do exactly what he'd just vowed he would not.

And yet... She studied his face, the impenetrable mask he wore. His eyes were guarded, giving nothing away. But when her gaze dropped to his hands on his desk, her impressions shifted. He'd clenched his fingers together, all the tension in his body centered on the tendons and bones of his hands.

What could be going on inside him that made control so imperative? She'd always seen him as arrogant, autocratic. In the two years she'd worked for him, she'd had to struggle constantly to hold her own, to stand her ground. Marrying him would make that battle ten times worse.

And yet... His gaze met hers unflinchingly as the grip of his hands tightened. Suddenly, her heart ached for him. And she knew, despite the sure peril ahead, what she would say.

"Yes, then," she said, nodding. "We'll marry."

A smile flashed on his face and was gone in an instant. Tension seemed to drain from his body. "Let me update you on my conversation with my attorney."

He launched into an explanation of the terms and conditions of their prenuptial agreement, his tone as impersonal as if he were discussing an upcoming corporate takeover. This was a union between a man and a woman, a joining together that should be done in love. She wished she could reach inside him somehow and shake that fierce reserve. But he'd withdrawn behind his barriers, unreachable.

She knew one way to shake him. She'd seen it last night when he'd leaned into her car to kiss her. He hadn't planned it, she was sure of that. Something other than his formidable mind had taken charge, pulled him to her.

What if she initiated a kiss? What if she rounded his desk right now and touched him? Slipped onto his lap, threaded her fingers into his hair and brought his mouth closer to hers? She'd gotten such a brief taste of him last night and the images had replayed themselves over and over in her mind as she'd tossed and turned in bed.

Closing her eyes, she raised her hands to her heated cheeks. She couldn't let her thoughts stray like this. A chaste marriage with Lucas would be difficult enough without fantasies to distract her.

"Allie, is something the matter?"

Her eyes flew open to see him staring at her intently. Thank God he couldn't read her mind. "I'm fine. What were you saying?"

"The prenuptial includes a settlement for you when the marriage terminates."

Planning the ending of their marriage so cold-heartedly only heightened her misgivings. But she was committed now, no matter how wrong it felt. "I don't need a settlement. You're already loaning me the twenty thousand."

"Giving, not loaning."

"I'm planning to pay it back."

"Don't be pigheaded about this, Allie. The money is yours, free and clear as of today. The rest will compensate you for the one to two years this process could take."

"It's not a process, Lucas. It's a marriage. An adoption of a child—a human being. You can't keep treating this as some sort of business transaction."

His fingers wrapped more tightly around the arms of his chair, the only indication she'd hit home with her comment. "You're right, of course. But I intend to give you the settlement, nonetheless."

"How much?" she asked warily.

"Two million." He said the amount casually, as if he were only offering her a couple hundred.

"You're crazy!" She leapt to her feet. "Totally nuts! That's too much, Lucas."

"The hell it is."

"I can't take that much." She shook her head. "No way."

He crossed his arms over his chest, his expression cold. "I'm damn well not budging on this, Allie."

She stared at him, completely flabbergasted. This was a man she'd seen go toe-to-toe with hardened businessmen, shaving millions off a deal if he felt the price was inflated. How could he justify giving her so much money?

But there was no arguing with him, at least for now. She'd have to find a way to refuse the money when the time came. She nodded her head in acquiescence.

"Give me your account number," he said, moving his chair up to the desk again. "Then we have to get on with the day. When's my first meeting?"

Lifting the laptop from his desk, she sank into her chair, trembling. Every time she thought she might have the upper hand, he backed her into a corner. How would she handle two years of this?

"The account number is in my purse. Why don't we go through your schedule first?"

He gave her a brusque nod, then she read off his commitments for the day. He told her what data he needed for his various meetings, reeling off the information with machine-gun rapidity. Somehow he seemed able to maintain his same businesslike demeanor while her hands shook on the keyboard, making one error after another as she typed.

When she finally escaped from his office to retrieve her purse, she had to give herself a moment to recover before going back inside. She sagged over her desk, leaning against it as she took a few deep breaths. Helen, who worked for one of Lucas's vice presidents, gave her a sympathetic smile. Allie responded in kind, although it was a weak effort.

Helen would know soon enough, and word would pass around the company from her and the handful of others Allie would tell. For now, she was just as glad to keep the news to herself, to have a chance to accustom herself to the shock.

Her phone buzzed, startling her. It was Lucas. Probably wanted to know what was keeping her. She picked up the phone. "Yes?"

"The account number?" he snapped out.

Struggling to hold onto her patience, she pulled out her checkbook and read off the appropriate digits. "Anything else?"

"Get on that church right away," he said.

"I will."

He fell silent and Allie assumed his mind had already shifted to his day's meetings. She was about to take the phone from her ear when he said, "Allie?"

The tentativeness of his tone surprised her. "Yes?"

Another long pause. "Thank you."

She didn't know what shocked her more—that he'd said it or that he sounded so genuinely grateful. "You're welcome." She lowered the phone back to its cradle.

She sat for a moment at her desk, trying to resolve the tumultuous feelings inside her. She was marrying Lucas Taylor, her boss. They would put on a facade of a happy marriage to allow him to adopt a child. She would be on her guard every moment against his overpowering personality, against her own inappropriate desires.

She understood the fear inside her, even the excitement. But one emotion roiling within her baffled her completely.

Joy.

After a day spent playing telephone tag with Lucas, Allie returned home with her nerves in a frazzle. She'd finally left a note on his desk about the church, giving up on actually seeing him face-to-face again that day. Now as she threw together a quick meal in the microwave, her gaze kept straying to the phone. She'd thought he might call her, to touch base, to compare notes on how the plans for their wedding were coming along. But it seemed now that he had her consent, he'd relegated her to one of those myriad compartments in his brain.

She had to call her sister and brother, had already put it off too long. She just didn't relish the inevitable questions and the answers she would have to fabricate. Not to mention she might miss a call from Lucas if she tied up the line.

She dawdled through her meal, eating little of it, then hurried downstairs to the apartment complex laundry room and started a load in the washer. When she returned, she quickly checked her answering machine— no message from Lucas. It was nearly eight; she couldn't put off her calls to her family any longer.

Her sister Sherril's husband answered the phone, giving Allie a few moments to compose what she planned to say. After assuring Sherril everything was fine both with her and their father, French, Allie asked, "Are you sitting down?"

Sherril's throaty laughter eased the tension in Allie's shoulders. "Lying down, actually. The baby's been playing the tom-toms on my spine."

Allie blurted out the news. "I'm getting married."

The silence stretched out uncomfortably before Sherril finally spoke. "How could you be getting married? You haven't even been dating anyone." Another pause. "Have you?"

Allie had realized before she picked up the phone she couldn't tell her sister the truth, not if she wanted to keep the predicament of their father's care to herself.

She could only hope the lie she'd concocted would sound believable.

"I'm marrying Lucas Taylor. My boss."

Sherril was quiet so long, Allie wondered if the connection had been broken. Finally she said, "I had no idea there was anything going on between you two."

Allie forced a laugh. "Neither did we. Just kind of sneaked up on us, I guess."

"Well...congratulations, then. When's the wedding?"

Allie braced herself for her sister's reaction. "End of September."

"What! I'll still be pregnant then," Sherril moaned. "Unless this beast decides to come early like his sister did. How am I going to find a whale-sized matron of honor dress?"

Allie smiled, pleased at Sherril's assumption she would be matron of honor. "I'm sure we can find something. Besides, this way, I have at least a hope of outshining you at the wedding."

"Allie, I gave up the crown of prettiest sister to you with my first set of stretch marks. Are you having it at the church?"

"Yes, the minister was able to fit us in, even at such short notice." Reverend Harmon had been so delighted at her news. Even now, Allie felt a stab of guilt at the lies she'd told him. "The reception will be at Lucas's estate."

Allie filled Sherril in on the remainder of the details, then begged her to pass on the news to their brother, Stephen. She simply didn't have the energy to spar with her brother, who still thought his baby sister needed his protection.

After she hung up the phone, Allie headed outside

to the apartment complex laundry room to shift her clothes to the dryer. As she fished quarters from her pocket to start the dryer, she realized even this mundane task would change when she moved to Lucas's expansive estate. No more lugging laundry down two flights of outside stairs in the winter rain or blistering summer sun. No tossing quarters into a jelly jar to have them ready for laundry day.

Would they wash their clothes together? Intermingling her life with Lucas's in such an ordinary way seemed terribly intimate. It made their upcoming marriage somehow more real, more valid.

Rattled by the notion, Allie left her clothes tumbling in the dryer and returned to her apartment. The flashing light on her answering machine sent her heart into overdrive—had Lucas called her after all? But it was only her brother Stephen, demanding she call him back tonight.

The last thing she needed was Stephen and his lectures. She'd committed herself to Lucas, to their marriage. Her brother's haranguing would only heighten her doubts.

Flipping on the TV, she watched a mindless cop show as she waited for her laundry to finish. Lucas never did call, but Stephen did, twice more. Allie resolutely ignored him each time.

With morning light spilling into his office, Lucas paced in agitation. In the week since he'd proposed marriage to Allie, he still hadn't regained his focus. Each day his preoccupation with his admin assistant grew until it had become a nearly unmanageable obsession.

When he first arrived in the mornings he was barely

able to pass her desk without touching her, without threading his fingers through her hair and tipping her head up to kiss her. He could hardly make it through their morning reviews, the urgency to round the desk and pull her into his arms so overwhelmed him. Sometimes her gaze met his as they worked together and he could see the wariness in her eyes. She had to sense his attraction for her.

His only recourse was to rush her through the recitation of his schedule, to hurry her out of his office. But her absence seemed to tantalize him more than her presence. Just the thought of her expressive green eyes set off a throbbing low in his body, a response he couldn't seem to control. Fantasies played themselves out in his mind—of him calling Allie into his office, tugging the dove-gray sleeveless shirt she wore today from the matching skirt, slipping his hand under it to cup her breast. Then lifting her to the desk, parting her legs and—

Damn, he had to get himself under control. He strode behind his desk and forced himself to sit. Locking his fingers together, he gripped them tightly on his desk.

If he couldn't keep his hands off her in these weeks before their wedding, how the hell would he do it once they were married? Once they were sharing his home, he wouldn't have a prayer if he didn't keep his rampant desires in line now. And he damn well intended to keep that promise.

Lucas dragged in a long breath and let it out. Most of the women he knew looked at sex the way he did—a necessary physical release. No messy emotions to get in the way. But Allie—still young and idealistic and full of hope—she might think physical intimacy meant more than it did. And the last thing he needed was Allie believing she was in love with him.

Unclenching his hands, he lifted a small Post-it square from the left side of his desk and repositioned it on the right. The note had been there all week, a glaring reminder of the upcoming wedding. On the pale-yellow square of paper, Allie had written down the name of the Methodist church in Fair Oaks and the time and date of the ceremony. *Reverend Frank Harmon,* she'd penned across the bottom of the note, the neat flowing loops of her script as feminine as the woman who wrote them.

A knock on his office door sent tension zinging up his spine. He dragged a folder to the center of his desk and opened it, dipping his head down to the stack of papers he should have been reviewing. "Enter."

Allie slipped inside, shutting the door behind her. As she crossed the office, her soft skirt rippled around her, shaping itself to the curves of her body. "Could we talk?" The faintest trace of irritation colored her tone.

He closed the folder with precise care. "Certainly."

She stood before his desk, shoulders thrown back. "You might be able to see our marriage as a cold-blooded business deal, but I can't. Even though we're not marrying for love, we're going to live together for the next two years. We ought to get to know each other better."

He struggled to focus on what she was saying, distracted by the way the late-morning sun lit her slender form. Would her skin feel warmer under that yellow glow? He shook off the image. "What do you want, Allie?"

"I want you to stop avoiding me."

"I haven't been avoiding you."

She just stared at him a moment, her expression telling him she knew a snow job when she heard one. "I want to spend some time with you, Lucas. I want a chance to get to know you a little better before the wedding."

It wasn't an unreasonable request, if you ignored the heat rippling through his body that urged him to get to know her much, much better. More time spent with her meant an even greater trial for his libido. But hell, he was a grown man. He ought to be able to give Allie what she wanted without breaking his promise of a platonic relationship.

She stood there, watching him, no doubt preparing her next argument if he turned her down. Lord, she was a hell of a fighter.

"What am I doing for lunch?" he asked her.

The question caught her off guard. She glanced around her as if seeking her laptop. "No meetings scheduled."

"I have one now," he said. "With you."

Her brilliant smile cut straight to his heart, setting off a flurry of unfamiliar emotions. Before he could catch his balance again, she'd moved around his desk and bent to put her arm around his shoulders. "Thank you," she murmured in his ear.

The warmth of her breath teased him, the nearness of her crumbled his good intentions. Before she could straighten, he'd curved his hands around her face, brought her mouth to his.

His fingers dove into her silky black hair, the softness against his skin a sweet torment. He brushed his mouth against hers, telling himself with each light touch to back off, to push her away. But when he'd kissed her a week ago, he'd had only the briefest taste. The memory of it had haunted him every night, stealing his sleep, infiltrating his dreams.

And he had to have more.

Chapter Four

Allie never should have touched him. In her delight over sharing lunch with Lucas, she'd let impulse take control. Now with him so near, with his breath fanning across her face as he stroked her lips with his, the snare of his passion wound around her.

She had to pull away. She took a step back to do just that when Lucas's mouth drifted from her lips, along her jaw to nuzzle in her ear. She swallowed back a moan, her pleasure easing out in a sigh instead. The hand he'd buried in her hair moved restlessly, its random pattern electric and breath-stealing.

Her own hands took their cue from him, gliding along the stiff shoulders of his jacket to the warm column of his throat. She wanted to ease her fingertips into his hair, explore his sensitive scalp as he did hers. She wanted to do more—to shift to stand in the V of his legs, to press her aching breasts against his chest.

She was lost. With so little effort, Lucas had taken over. And yet she had only to take another step back, to straighten and tug herself away and he would let her go. He had to let her go.

Drawing in a trembling breath, Allie struggled to regain her strength, her will. She slid her hands from Lucas's throat, pressed her palms against his shoulders. The instant he felt the pressure of her hands against him, he released her so that she nearly stumbled as she backed away.

He sprang from his chair, turning away from her. Facing the window, he pressed both palms against the glass, arms stiff with tension. "Hell."

She heard a tremor in the softly spoken word. Raising a shaky hand, she smoothed her hair from her face. "I'm sorry."

His head swiveled toward her, his eyes blazing. "What the devil do you have to be sorry for?"

"Because I…" Her stomach knotted, cutting off the words. She took a breath. "I shouldn't have touched you."

For a long moment, he just stared at her. Then he pushed away from the window. "No you shouldn't. Because I damn well can't seem to control…" Stabbing his fingers through his thick dark hair in agitation, he raised his gaze to hers. "I'm the one who should apologize. You did nothing wrong. I took advantage…hell."

She'd seen Lucas angry, seen him throw on a cloak of intimidation that drove fear into the hearts of his adversaries, but she'd never seen him this way—flustered, uncertain, off-balance. His unsettling vulnerability set off a chord inside Allie, an unexpected tenderness.

Which sent her thoughts marching in a perilous direction. She edged away from him, headed for the door. She could feel his eyes on her every step, but couldn't quite meet his gaze. "Is lunch still...do you still want to...?"

"When are my appointments finished?"

"Twelve-thirty." She chanced a quick glance at him. The softness she'd seen before in him had gone, replaced by his usual icy calm.

"Twelve-thirty, then."

He retrieved his chair and lowered himself into it. She reached for the door.

"Allie."

The gentleness of his tone drew her back around. Arms across her middle, she faced him. Something flickered in his eyes, emotions that seemed to struggle to the surface before sinking again into the mystery that was Lucas Taylor.

He dropped his gaze, shuffled papers into the file folder on his desk. "I'll need that production cost spreadsheet for the eleven o'clock sales meeting."

He'd shut himself off again, reverting to the businessman. He so easily suppressed the emotions that still had her in turmoil.

Irritation gnawed at her. "How many copies?" she snapped out.

"Ten should do it."

He still kept his gaze fixed on the file folder as if it revealed some crucial secret. Despite the bland neutrality of his expression, tension gripped him, holding him so tightly Allie's heart ached for him.

Her irritation faded away. "I'll have them ready for you in ten minutes."

She slipped from his office, moved to sit at her desk.

As she connected her laptop with her desktop computer, she tried to untangle the confusion inside her. But when it came to Lucas Taylor, nothing was simple.

With a sigh, Allie brought up the spreadsheet program and with an effort of will, threw herself into her work.

At exactly twelve-thirty, Lucas returned from the sales meeting and strode to her desk. "Let's go," he demanded.

In the process of transferring figures from the quarterly marketing report to a spreadsheet, Lucas's command splintered Allie's hard-won concentration. She pressed the wrong key and deleted the last hour's work. "Damn!"

She glared up at Lucas, then quickly clicked the Undo command. Banging at the keyboard, she saved her work and set her laptop on standby. With an angry jerk she pulled open her desk drawer and grabbed her purse.

She seethed silently in the elevator. He seemed oblivious to her anger. When they reached the ground floor, he laid his hand lightly at the small of her back and guided her through the lobby.

"We'll visit my jeweler after lunch." He opened the lobby door for her, stepping aside to let her go first. "We haven't selected rings yet. I'd rather have you there since I don't know your preferences."

The midday heat scorched her in the first few steps outside the building's air-conditioned comfort. She couldn't hold in her agitation an instant longer. Whirling to stand in his path, she stopped his forward progress.

"My *preference* is that you treat me with a modicum

of respect and courtesy. My *preference* is that you remember I'm not a serf you can order to do your bidding.''

He gazed down at her, his expression baffled. "What are you talking about?"

She clenched her jaw and looked away a moment to gather her patience, then she returned her gaze to his. "If you hadn't noticed, I was working in there, doing your work as a matter of fact. In the time I've been employed by you I've put up with your arrogance because you were my boss.''

She pointed a finger at him, prodded him in the chest for emphasis. "You're still my boss. But if we go through with this crazy idea of a marriage, I want you to ask politely, not bark out an order.''

Before she could take another breath, his hand flew up to capture hers. He held it against his chest, his lips thinning with what looked like the genesis of anger. For an instant, he was her father, his rage at her impertinence a storm brewing inside him. It had happened every time she'd stood up to him, asserted herself as an individual. And even knowing this was Lucas, not her father, she couldn't help the first tendrils of insecurity winding around her stomach.

Even as she tensed for the anticipated explosion, his mouth relaxed, his lips softening and curving into a faint smile. "I'm sorry,'' he said, his thumb moving against the back of her hand. "I'm too much a creature of habit.''

Relief flooded her, even as her body responded to the stroking of his thumb, to his gaze fixed briefly on her mouth. She supposed she should pull her hand away, but it felt so pleasant enfolded in his, resting lightly against his chest. He'd worn a pale-gray shirt today and she imagined gliding her palm along the crisp smoothness, shaping the musculature underneath.

"Thank you," she said, not sure what she was thanking him for. The sun beat down on them, rivaling the heat Lucas's touch had set off in her. "I guess we should go."

She thought he would release her hand, but he kept it in his, interlacing his fingers with hers. Her bare arm rubbed against the sleeve of his suit jacket as he kept pace with her.

Up ahead the parking lot steamed in the brilliant sunlight. When they reached his silver Mercedes, he paused before pulling out his keys, raised her hand again to his chest. "It's been a long time since I've held a woman's hand."

His comment startled her. She knew he hadn't been without a woman for long; he'd been dating someone as recently as late spring. The woman had come into the office a half dozen times, a tall edgy blonde who apparently owned a high-power consulting firm in downtown Sacramento. Allie tried to remember if she'd ever seen Lucas holding the woman's hand. She could only recall the blonde's stunning looks, how striking a couple she and Lucas had made.

Yet another puzzle piece that didn't seem to fit. Lucas brushed his lips against her knuckles, sending a tremor through her, then let go to fish the car keys out of his pocket. He opened the passenger-side door, helping her in before rounding the car to the driver's side.

As they pulled out of the lot, Allie remembered what Lucas had said about the jeweler. "We don't need rings," she told him.

He didn't even look her way, just glanced at the

rearview mirror as he merged into traffic on Douglas Boulevard. "We're getting rings."

"I'll just have to return mine when we...after."

"You'll keep it."

Along with that ridiculous amount of money he was insisting she take. "Then we'll just get plain bands. Something inexpensive."

Brow arched, he shot his gaze her way, then returned his attention to his driving. Allie sighed, realizing he might have agreed to treat her with courtesy, but it wouldn't change his attempts to run her life. She'd have to be constantly vigilant, or he might smother her very identity as her father had done for all those years.

Lucas saw the surprise in Allie's face when they pulled up to the tiny Mexican restaurant he'd decided on for lunch. She'd expected something pricey and up-scale, more like the Cliff House where they'd dined the night he'd proposed to her. *Cocina Caldera* was nearly a hole-in-the-wall by comparison, but the food was good, the service excellent. That he had a connection to the owner, Teresa Caldera, that he felt a certain comfort here he felt nowhere else was immaterial.

When they stepped inside the packed restaurant, Teresa Caldera and her daughter Inez greeted Lucas by name as they hurried by with steaming plates. As he and Allie waited for a table, Lucas shifted uneasily, wondering what Allie thought of the place, wondering if by being here he somehow revealed too much of his past.

Suddenly anxious to leave, he said, "It's too crowded. We'll try somewhere else."

She smiled up at him. "I'm not in any hurry. This place smells wonderful."

By now they'd edged their way up to the cash register where Teresa rang up a sale. The stout woman, her dark hair threaded with gray, grinned up at him. *"Hola, guapo, ¿Cómo estás?"*

"Bien," he replied in automatic response to the familiar greeting.

Teresa gave Allie a pointed look, and Lucas felt suddenly awkward, like a teenager introducing his girlfriend to his parents for the first time. This was the only time he'd brought anyone but a business associate to the restaurant.

"This is Alison Dickenson, my administrative assistant. Allie, this is Teresa Caldera."

The two women shook hands, then Teresa rushed off to pick up another order. Inez came to seat them and Lucas sank into the booth in relief.

As they scanned their menus, the crowd thinned out and the din quieted. Lucas could feel Allie's gaze on him. He raised his eyes to hers.

"What?"

She shrugged. "You didn't introduce me as your fiancée."

Of course she'd noticed. "It slipped my mind."

She eyed him in frank disbelief. "Nothing slips your mind, Lucas."

"Teresa would have made a big deal over it. I didn't want her fussing."

"You must know her well to have her fuss over you like that."

Damn Allie and her observant nature. "I eat here often," Lucas said evenly as the plastic edges of the menu bit into his palms. "Teresa has a way of making her regulars family."

Lucas could see she wanted to push the issue of Teresa. He set the menu down. "Are you ready to order?" Without waiting for her to answer, he signaled Inez.

Out of habit, he ordered in Spanish and Inez joked about his atrocious accent as she always did. She insisted he introduce Allie, her dark brow rising when he described Allie as "his good friend." No doubt Inez would be comparing notes with Teresa back in the kitchen.

The questions seemed to pile up in Allie's green eyes. While they waited for their food, Lucas kept Allie busy with questions about work, querying her about when she'd have the month-end reports ready.

When Inez brought their lunch, Lucas dove into his fajitas, focusing on piling strips of beef, red pepper and onion onto the flour tortillas. From the corner of his eye he could see Allie watching him.

"Is there something wrong with your *molé?*" he asked. "We can send it back."

"The *molé* is fine," Allie said. "But we're kind of defeating the purpose here. The whole point to having lunch together was to get to know each other. We never will if we keep talking about work."

He set down his fork. "What do you want to know?"

She smiled at him across the table. "I'd just like to learn a little more about you."

Wariness crept into the pit of his stomach. "Like what?"

"Where you grew up, where your parents live, if you have brothers and sisters."

Such ordinary questions, easy enough for most people to answer. But for him, they opened a can of worms he had no intention of opening. "I grew up in the Sacramento area. I have no brothers and sisters. My parents are dead.''

He could see the sympathy in her face. ''I'm sorry. How long have they been gone?''

''A long time.'' To cut short her inquiry, he turned the question around to her. ''What about your family?''

''A brother and a sister. Both married, both have kids. I have four nieces and nephews with another on the way. My mom...'' She looked away a moment, and grief flashed across her face. ''She died a few years ago. My dad...he lives in Reno.''

''French Dickenson, right? *Forbes* did quite a write-up on him, what...ten years ago?''

''Twelve.'' Her gaze dropped to her plate and she ran the tines of her fork through the thick *molé* sauce. ''He was very proud of that article.''

The motion of Allie's wrist as it bent and straightened, bent and straightened, snagged Lucas's attention. He could imagine that same mesmerizing movement against his own body. Shaking the image off, he asked, ''Is he still running Postal Express?''

Her hand froze. She kept her eyes on her plate. ''No. He's retired.''

Lucas could see something in her face.... Sorrow? Regret? He wanted to reach across the table, lay a soothing hand against her cheek. He squelched the impulse. ''Will he be coming to the wedding?''

Now she did look up at him, eyes wide. ''No!'' She smiled, gesturing with her hand as if to take away the vehemence of her denial. ''Traveling is difficult for him. He's not in the best of health. Sherril, Stephen and I visit him on Sundays.''

Now it was his turn to be curious. He tried to remember what he might have read in the business-trade magazines about French Dickenson's retirement. If there had been mention, it must have been small enough to have passed his notice.

"I'll meet him later, then," Lucas said.

She nodded, then bent her head to her lunch. She pushed more of it around on her plate than she actually ate. By the time Inez came to bring the check, Allie had slid the nearly full plate aside.

She laced her fingers together and rested them on the table, tipped her head up to him. "So you won't have anyone to invite to the wedding. No family, I mean."

Across the room, Teresa stood at the register. She smiled broadly, speculation clear in her lined face as she watched him with Allie. There were people he could invite—Teresa, her brother Guillermo, Inez. Until this moment it hadn't crossed his mind. Until this moment, it hadn't occurred to him how hurt Teresa would be to be excluded. He'd gone off to Tahoe to wed Carol and Teresa still nursed that pain. It had been enough of a disappointment that his chosen bride hadn't been Inez.

Yet, by inviting the Calderas, Lucas risked opening a door to his past he'd long ago nailed shut. How would he explain to Allie what Teresa and Guillermo were to him without telling her the rest? Only by flat lies which his foster mother would never be party to.

Damn, he never should have brought Allie to *Cocina Caldera.* What had he been thinking?

Glancing at the check, Lucas tossed down a twenty and rose abruptly to his feet. "The jeweler's expecting us."

He put out his hand to help Allie from her seat, conscious all the time of Teresa's eyes on him. As he followed Allie from the restaurant, he waved to Teresa and Inez, glad to escape from their scrutiny.

Allie looked thoughtful as she sat beside him in the Benz, as if she was considering all the evidence and waited for it to click into place. The leather-wrapped steering wheel went slick with the sweat of his palms.

"They seem like such nice people," Allie said finally.

"Yes, they are." The questions were coming, he could feel them ready to beat at him, ready to expose the hidden past. Not that he would answer them, but just being asked was painful enough. He sucked in a breath and held it.

"Do you think we could have the reception there?" she asked, her tone offhand. "Instead of at your estate?"

The innocent, simple query pulled the air back out of his lungs. It was the perfect solution, one he should have thought of himself. It was a way to include the Calderas without making an issue of his relationship with them.

A traffic light up ahead went yellow and he stepped on the brake. He glanced over at Allie, looked for some inner knowledge she kept to herself. He saw only her frank open gaze.

Gratitude welled up in him, mingled with a joy he didn't know how to handle. Somehow, Allie knew what the Calderas meant to him without asking for the details.

He swallowed against the surge of emotion. "Teresa would love to host a wedding dinner. I'll arrange it when we get back to the office."

"I can take care of it," Allie offered.

"I'll do it," Lucas said brusquely. "I'm familiar

with their specials. I'll know what to order." And it would give him a chance to talk things over with Teresa, to maintain the secret of his years in foster care with her.

Allie nodded her acquiescence. The light turned green and he drove on. He flexed his hands on the wheel as he tried to tuck away the emotions Allie managed to stir in him. This beautiful young woman, at once gentle and determined, posed more peril to his neat compartmentalized life than he ever would have expected.

Thunderstruck, Allie stared down at the ring the jeweler held out to her. "No. No way." She gestured at the massive solitaire, at what must have been a ten-carat diamond set in platinum. "That's way too much, Lucas."

Lucas's mouth set in a stubborn line. "I can easily afford it."

"I'm sure you can." Allie glanced up at the jeweler. A spare, sandy-haired man of indeterminate age, he remained silent as he offered the ring for her approval.

She narrowed her gaze against the brilliant light set off by the blue-white stone. "Lucas, it's an incredible ring, but I'd feel a little…ridiculous wearing a diamond that big."

Faint color rose in his cheeks and Allie realized she'd offended him. She laid her hand lightly on his arm. "It's gorgeous. But I'd truly love something a bit…simpler. Less ostentatious."

He wanted to continue the argument; she could see it in the set of his jaw. She thought about the strange mixture of emotions she'd seen in him at lunch.

She knew why he wanted such a showy ring. Despite

his cold and autocratic image, Lucas was a generous man by nature. She'd seen it in his lavish annual bonuses to the staff, in the godawful amount of money he was insisting on paying her as a settlement. This outrageously expensive ring was his way of expressing his generosity of character; he didn't know any other way.

She turned to the jeweler. "Do you have something more delicate? More feminine?"

The jeweler whisked away the solitaire without comment, no sign on his impassive face that he regretted the loss of what had to be a sizeable commission. Setting the ring back into the case, the jeweler scanned the rows of wedding sets before plucking one from the ranks.

He held the ring box out to Allie. "Perhaps this one?"

"Oh," Allie sighed as she reached for the rings. She cupped the box in her hand, gazing down at the delicately wrought rings, gold filigree and diamonds flowing in a sweetly feminine design. "Yes, this is perfect."

She looked up at Lucas, saw the conflicting play of emotions in his face. Was he unhappy she'd chosen a different ring? Angry that she wouldn't cooperate with his choice?

He took the ring box from her and she half expected him to return it to the jeweler. Instead he slipped the engagement ring from the deep-blue velvet, set the box aside and took her left hand.

His gray gaze on her face, he slid the ring onto her finger. It went on too easily, would probably have to be sized to fit her, but it looked so exquisite she hated to give it up. And the way Lucas's warm fingers enfolded her hand, she wanted to stand there forever, her gaze locked with his.

The jeweler cleared his throat. "I can have those sized for you this afternoon, have them ready by six."

Flustered, feeling the heat rise in her cheeks, Allie tugged away from Lucas. Her hands trembling, she pulled the ring off and fitted it back into the box. She glanced up at the jeweler, saw his pleased smile.

"This is the best part of my job." The man beamed as he set aside the rings. "Especially when a couple is as in love as you two obviously are."

She almost shook her head to refute the jeweler's assessment. Because certainly they weren't in love. This marriage between her and Lucas had nothing to do with devotion to one another. Yet that was the illusion they intended to convey, and somehow the jeweler had seen the facsimile of love in them.

She stole a glance at her husband-to-be, tried to read the thoughts behind the implacable lines of his face. The raw angle of his jaw, the slash of his cheekbone told her less than nothing. If he felt awkward or embarrassed by the jeweler's assumption, he didn't show it.

As she gazed at him, a yearning rose in Allie, a desire not quite fully formed. There existed deep within this man something so precious it far outweighed the value of the gaudy stone he'd wanted to buy her. She ached to delve inside him, to take a breath like a pearl diver and bring the priceless treasure to light. An impossible task. A man as formidable as Lucas had more barriers than the most protected fortress, more twists and turns than the most torturous maze.

And then, even as she watched, the steel-gray of his eyes softened, ever so slightly. He reached for her hand, lifting it to his mouth. He brushed his lips across her knuckles, a whisper of a touch. Then, before he released her, he paused, eyes shut, his warm lips pressed against her skin.

In that instant she would have given anything, everything, even the exquisite ring about to become the token of their marriage, to know what emotions stirred inside him.

Then he let go and with the loss of contact, the marvelous, precarious moment was lost.

Chapter Five

Lucas stood motionless in the center of his expansive living room, staring out the windows overlooking the lake that marked the back boundary of his property. With the arrival of September, the days had seemed anxious to end earlier and earlier. As 7:00 p.m. dragged into 7:30, the sun teased the tops of the oak trees off in the distance.

She would be here any minute. Their Saturday-afternoon wedding would be a week from today, and Allie had yet to visit his house. Tonight she would be bringing over some of her things, would take the first steps in claiming one of the guest rooms as her own.

It was ridiculous that he should be nervous. Ever since the episode at the jeweler's when he'd so badly misjudged the style of ring she would want, uncertainty about anything to do with Allie was his constant companion. Now he worried that she would hate his house, that the moment she stepped inside, her face would fall and dismay would be obvious in her expressive eyes.

Stress set his stomach churning, making him sorry he'd eaten that quickly slapped-together sandwich an hour ago. He'd wanted Allie to join him for dinner and had asked his filipina housekeeper, Mrs. Vasquez, to make something special. Knowing his fiancée would be sharing the meal with him, Mrs. Vasquez had gone into a culinary frenzy, preparing two filipino favorites—a massive bowl of *pancit,* with *brazos* for dessert. The fragrance of the *pancit* and its sautéed noodles, vegetables and shrimp still lingered.

But the piled-high bowl of *pancit* sat untouched in the refrigerator. Allie had called at six, sounding frazzled and rushed and had begged off dinner. She was running late, would have to grab something on the run, didn't want him to wait for her. The bite of disappointment had surprised him, threatened to rouse old memories of childhood hurts, of carefully prepared meals left uneaten.

He brushed away those memories now as the sun edged a bit closer to the lattice of oak tree branches. He'd been a lost child then, powerless over the one adult in his life who meant so much to him. To compare that to the inconvenience of missing dinner with Allie was ludicrous.

Yet his fingernails had dug half moons into his palms. He shook the tension from his hands, shoving them into the pockets of his khakis. He twisted a little, left and right, then rotated his shoulders. Despite the perfectly controlled climate in his air-conditioned house, his polo shirt clung to his body, damp with perspiration.

He took one step toward the tall windows overlooking the lake when the sputter of a badly tuned engine turned him around. He spotted Allie's Buick winding up the drive, slowing as it approached the house. He strode quickly to the front door, wrenching it open and hurrying down the stairs.

By the time he reached Allie's car, she'd opened the door herself and stood looking over the top of the Buick toward the house. She stared at it silently, her gaze moving along the wraparound porch, along the second-story windows to the barely visible lake beyond. Lucas took a deep breath in an attempt to quiet the rapid beating of his heart. He couldn't understand his reaction. Why was it so damn important to him that she like his house?

She turned to him, smiling, her eyes bright with pleasure. "It's beautiful, Lucas. It's a dream house."

He couldn't have stopped his answering smile to save his life. The joy that rocketed through him at her approval threw him off-balance. He couldn't think of what to say in response, especially with her green eyes fixed on him. His "Thank-you" came out with stiff formality.

Grabbing her purse, she swung the car door shut, then opened the back seat. "These wouldn't fit in the suitcases." She reached in for a pile of clothes on hangers, then jiggled the keys wedged in her hand. "The rest is in the trunk."

He took the keys from her and unlocked the trunk, pocketing the keys. One way or another, he was going to find a way to get her another car. Maybe he'd force the issue by not returning her keys. Her arms around a thick stack of clothes, Allie waited while he retrieved the three bulging suitcases from the trunk.

"Lead the way," she said, smiling up at him.

At the sight of her tipped-up face, the sweet curve of her mouth, her vivid green eyes, heat spiraled throughout his body. Even with her hair escaping her ponytail, her face washed clean of makeup, in her well-worn tank top and jeans, she couldn't disguise her sensuality. He ached to touch her, to throw aside their burdens and draw her to him. He wanted her body against his, wanted to relieve the pressure in his groin with her softness.

He gasped in a breath and turned away from her abruptly. ''Your room is upstairs.''

Allie watched Lucas stride up the porch steps, his body ramrod straight. In an instant, his mercurial moods appeared to have shifted from uncertainty to joy to a blatant attraction she couldn't deny. In the space from one heartbeat to the next, he had cast her into complete confusion.

He waited for her in the foyer, stepped way back as she entered the house. He nudged the door shut, then paused again while she perused his living room. Just as he had outside, he gave her an expectant look, as if he waited for her judgment, almost like a child searching for approval.

Struggling to resolve the paradox that was Lucas, Allie turned away from him to gaze out the windows on the other side of the room. A lake glowed in the last of the sunlight, a dock on its near side, massive blue oaks on its other shore.

A private lake. A fairy-tale house. And Lucas Taylor, the handsome prince she would share it with. The enormity of it threatened to overwhelm her.

Forcing a smile, she turned back to him. ''Do you swim in the lake? Does it have fish?''

Whatever uncertainty she'd seen before in him had vanished. "Yes to both," he said. "I keep it stocked with trout and bass."

She laughed. "Your very own lake. That's amazing."

He gestured with the suitcases toward the stairs. "There's a room adjoining yours. I thought we could make that the nursery."

A nursery. In the crazy whirl of details she'd had to handle in the past few weeks, she'd boxed away in her mind the real reason he'd asked her to marry him. To allow him to adopt a child.

Now, as she followed him up the stairs, she tried to picture a youngster in this pristine and formal house. Stopping to look over the railing of the landing to the living room below, she saw hazard after hazard in Lucas's exquisite home.

Her arms growing tired with their load, she rested them on the railing. "How old a child had you planned to adopt?"

He hesitated before answering. "My attorney has been looking for an infant." He set down the suitcases, opened a door. "Your room is here."

She ran her gaze along the curve of stairs, then out the back windows where she could see the edge of the lake's near shore. "Then you'll have some time to set things up."

She turned to see him standing between the suitcases, his arms rigid at his sides. "Set things up?"

Sidling past him into the room, she dumped the stack of clothes on the bed. "A child safety gate on the top of the stairs, something to fence off the lake."

She might as well have been speaking in Greek for

all the comprehension he showed in his face. "Why would I fence off the lake?"

She went to retrieve a suitcase, brought it over to the double oak dresser at the foot of the bed. "Once the baby's walking, you'll want to restrict him or her to safe areas. That means fencing off the lake or providing an enclosed play yard. Child latches on the cupboards in the kitchen, covers for the outlets."

Lifting the suitcase to the top of the dresser, she opened it and began to empty the contents into drawers. She looked over her shoulder at Lucas, feeling a little awkward having him watch her fill the drawers with panties and bras. But he seemed a million miles away, his eyes downcast.

Sliding a drawer shut, she moved to where he still stood in the doorway. "It's a lot to think about, isn't it?"

His head swung up, an intense light in his eyes. "I haven't thought about it at all. I never thought past getting a child."

He spoke of the adoption as if it were an acquisition, like buying a car or a piece of property. Surely he couldn't be that cold. "Lucas." She placed her hand on his arm, momentarily distracted by the feel of his warm skin, the flex and pull of the muscles beneath. "Have you truly thought this out? Are you genuinely ready to adopt a child? It's a lifetime commitment—is it really what you want?"

She knew immediately the question was a mistake; could see it in the storm of emotion that played across his face. First anger, then a haughty arrogance. If it hadn't been for one telltale gesture, she would have believed he was in a rage over her impertinence.

He looked away. For just an instant his gray eyes

couldn't meet hers and doubt held sway. Then he fixed his hard gaze on her, his jaw set, his expression harsh.

"It's not your place to ask that question," he said, biting out the words. Then he turned away, and she heard his footsteps sounding along the landing, the opening and slamming of a door.

With a sigh, Allie shoved aside the clothes on the bed and lowered herself to the edge. She felt taut as a bowstring, aching from the inside out. She ached for Lucas and the pain he wouldn't share, ached for the child that would soon come into this house to live with him. Every uncertainty she'd had about the madness of their upcoming wedding assailed her now, urged her to break away while there was still time.

But nothing had changed. Not her need for money, not the commitment she'd made. Lucas had already paid her debts; how could she not follow through? Even if she promised to repay the money, it wouldn't be right to renege on her part of the bargain.

She would have to follow through. There was really no other choice.

Heart-sore, she rose, looked around her at the room. The double bed and two nightstands filled one wall, the dresser and a small dressing table the opposite wall. To her left were a walk-in closet and a door to the bathroom beyond; to her right a door that must lead into the nursery.

He'd furnished the room plainly. Plantation shutters covered the windows flanking the bed, the oak dresser and nightstands were simply made, without ornamentation. Perhaps he sensed she'd want to impose her own personality on the room and had left it to her to add the final touches.

With some trepidation, she moved toward the nurs-

ery door, wondering if that room would be as featureless. Easing open the door, she poked her head inside,
saw a crib and a changing table, a small white dresser
and a toy chest. The crib had been made up with sheets
and sported a pastel comforter; a nondescript mobile
hung above it.

She moved around the foot of the crib, set the mobile
spinning with her finger. She imagined a baby sleeping
here, snug under the comforter, warm and loved.
Smoothing a hand over the covers, she tried to picture
Lucas lifting the baby in his arms, holding it close.
Instead she recalled him standing in the doorway of her
room, stiff and prickly, with nothing soft about him.

Turning to go, her gaze fell on something propped
in the corner of the crib. Tattered and stained, a ragged
bear leaned against the crib slats, its eyes blank brown
buttons. Its left foot was scorched and a little stuffing
had leaked out. As bedraggled as it was, the stuffed
toy begged Allie to pick it up.

As she reached for it she wondered if the housekeeper had put it here. Perhaps the well-loved toy had
been a grandchild's and the woman knew the room
needed something real, something personal. It surprised
Allie that Lucas would have allowed it to stay.

Turning the bear over, Allie found a frayed tag still
attached by a few threads. Flipping over the tag, her
heart squeezed tight in her chest. Scrawled on the tag,
nearly illegible, was the letter *L.*

L for Lucas. It was his bear. Tears tightened her
throat, brimmed in her eyes. Lucas had played with this
bear as a boy, had saved it all these years. And now,
when he seemed to know nothing about children, how
to love them, how to raise them, he knew at least this

much—that a child needed something like this bear to hold on to for comfort.

She set the stuffed toy back into the crib where she'd found it, brushed away the tears that had spilled down her cheeks. The sound of nearby footsteps startled her and she realized they came from the room next door, Lucas's room. She heard his door open again, then close, then Lucas walking along the landing toward her room.

Not wanting him to find her in the nursery, she quickly slipped out, shutting the door behind her. Although her bedroom door was still open, he rapped on the doorjamb without coming inside. "Allie?"

"Yes." She smoothed away the rest of the moisture from her cheeks. "Come in."

He stepped inside, his expression wary, his gray eyes turbulent. He stood stiffly, his wide shoulders stretching the knit of his pale-gray polo shirt, the raw lines of his face set. Feature by feature, he wasn't a handsome man, but taken as a whole he was devastating. Allie fought to resolve the image of the man before her with the stuffed bear she'd found in the nursery and could not.

She was completely unprepared for what he had to say. "I'm sorry."

She shook her head slowly. "For…?"

"What I said before. That you had no right…" He tightened his hands into fists, then uncurled them with effort. "You have every right. You're to be my wife."

The words were stilted and awkwardly spoken, but she could see the effort it took him to say them. She smiled, gestured to the suitcases, the clothes piled on the bed. "I guess I should get back to this."

He stepped inside the room. "Can I help?"

"No, I…" She laughed. "Yes, please. I'm so used to me helping you in the office, it seems strange for you to…"

"This isn't the office. You don't work for me here." With one finger on her chin, he tipped her face up. "You understand that, don't you? You will be my wife in every way but one."

She stood there, stunned, trying to absorb what he'd said. "But only until the adoption is final," she reminded him.

He kept his gaze steady on her face. "Yes. Until then."

Turning away from her, he reached for the suitcases still outside the room, brought them in. "Now, what can I do?"

Allie leaned against the kitchen island, surveying the large room as Lucas prepared coffee. Miles of granite countertops, acres of rich oak cupboards, gleaming pots and pans hanging from wrought-iron hooks—the room made her own pint-sized kitchen seem like a broom closet.

As he measured out coffee and water, Lucas stood with his back to her, the display of muscles under his shirt tempting her to touch. Working together in the close quarters of her room, watching him handling her clothes as he hung her dresses, blouses and slacks in the closet, had tautened the sensual thread that always seemed to run between them.

Once when she'd looked over her shoulder at him, she'd caught him with one of her silk shirts in his hands, fingers caressing the delicate fabric while he stared thoughtfully at her. He'd looked away quickly, leaving her with her heart beating crazily, fingers trembling as she continued to stow her things in the dresser.

Now he turned to face her, leaning against the kitchen counter while the coffee brewed. "What do you take in your coffee?"

The simple query seemed layered with meaning. There was nothing intimate about a cup of coffee, but in that charged atmosphere, he might as well be asking her preferences in bed.

Elbows resting on the granite-topped island, Allie crossed her arms over her middle. "Two sugars." She laughed softly. "We're marrying in less than a week and we don't even know how we each take our coffee."

"Black," he said, fingers curled around the edge of the counter. "And strong."

As his gaze locked with hers, the very air seemed to thicken, to caress her skin. She broke the visual contact, stared down at her hands as if they held the secrets of the universe.

When she looked up again, he'd turned away, opening the refrigerator to retrieve two bowls. Setting them on the counter by the coffeemaker, he unwrapped the plastic from the bowls and set a spoon inside each one.

"It's called *brazos*," he said, bringing the bowls over to the island. "Custard covered with meringue. One of Mrs. Vasquez's specialties."

"Mrs. Vasquez?"

"My housekeeper. She's from the Philippines." He turned to pull two mugs from the cupboard. "She's been with me for several years, but you can choose your own housekeeper if you'd rather."

Mrs. Vasquez had been with him for years, was undoubtedly a loyal employee. Allie knew what loyalty meant to Lucas, had seen him time and again reward employee devotion to TaylorMade with salary increases and bonuses. Yet he'd offered to dismiss his housekeeper if Allie wished it.

His offhand tone implied it didn't matter either way. But she saw the stillness in his body; saw how tightly he gripped the mugs he'd just taken down.

"I'm sure I'll love her."

He relaxed then, set the mugs down on the counter. "Did you want to eat in here or in the living room?"

"The living room." She picked up the bowls. "Shall I take these out?"

He nodded as he poured the coffee. Allie carried the bowls to the living room, set them on the table next to the sofa.

She'd gotten only a brief look at the room when she'd first come into the house. It was obviously professionally decorated, with oatmeal-colored Berber carpet, a sleek taupe sectional sofa, occasional tables in glowing oak. Subdued track lighting illuminated the artwork on the walls, pricey lithographs and original oils.

She didn't doubt everything here was the best money could buy. But there was nothing of Lucas in any of the furnishings, no touch to make the room seem real. It all coordinated perfectly, as if order and structure mattered more than making this place a home.

Except for one small watercolor squeezed between two floor-to-ceiling bookcases. Allie crossed the room for a closer look, smiled in delight at the vivid splashes of color that filled the neatly framed piece. The staid mahogany that surrounded the abstract image seemed barely able to enclose its energy.

She looked for a signature in the lower right hand

corner of the painting and saw with a shock the familiar, hastily scribbled *L.*

She turned to Lucas when he entered with the coffee. "This is wonderful." She gestured at the watercolor. "I didn't know you painted."

"I don't." He set one mug on the table with the *brazos,* color rising in his face. "Sit. Your coffee's getting cold."

He seemed embarrassed by the uncharacteristic burst of creativity, which only heightened Allie's curiosity. She returned to the sofa, slipped off her shoes and took a seat. Curling her legs under her, she picked up her bowl.

Lucas remained standing. His strong hands curved around his mug, he didn't drink, didn't pick up his bowl to eat. He just watched her.

Feeling edgy under his appraisal, Allie took a bite of the *brazos.* The delectable sweetness caught her off guard and she closed her eyes, moaning in appreciation as the meringue and custard melted on her tongue.

"It's delicious," she said as the luscious taste faded. She opened her eyes, smiling at Lucas.

The intensity of his gaze sent sensation lancing through her. She had to force herself to drag in her next breath, to quiet the trembling in her hands.

She tipped her head down to her bowl, focusing on another bite. "I'd love to know how to make this," she said, dipping in her spoon for more.

He still hadn't taken a sip of coffee, just stood holding it in his hands. "I'm sure Mrs. Vasquez would be glad to show you."

"It must be nice having a housekeeper to cook for you. Especially when you entertain."

"I don't entertain."

She blinked in surprise. "Never?"

He shrugged. "I don't like bringing clients into my home."

That she knew, since she usually made the arrangements at a local restaurant. "You must have friends who visit."

"My attorney, John, has dinner with me from time to time."

His attorney...that was his only friend? "And when you date—"

"I never bring them home."

"Never?" The realization stunned her. "Then I'm the first woman—"

"Besides Mrs. Vasquez and the professional decorator you're the only woman I've had here at the house."

She tried to absorb what he'd said. He owned this big, beautiful house, never entertained, scarcely brought friends here to visit. She looked around her at the stark living room and saw something new in its featureless perfection—loneliness.

The brilliant hues of the watercolor caught her eye. "When did you paint that?"

Lucas swung his head toward the painting, his jaw tightening. "A long time ago."

An urgency arose in Allie, to touch him, to soothe him. "Lucas."

He turned to face her. Despite the danger she invited by having him nearer, Allie patted the seat beside her. "Come sit with me."

For a moment he didn't move, then he set aside his coffee and lowered himself beside her with a sigh. She put down her bowl, laid her hand on his arm.

It seemed the most natural thing in the world that he

turn to her, that he pull her to him. She slid her hands around his waist as he wrapped his arms around her. She reveled in the warmth of his broad chest against her cheek, the feel of his powerful arms around her. And although he didn't completely relax, she could feel at least some of his tension released with a long exhalation of breath.

His heart thrummed against her ear, a steady beat. She tipped her head back to look up at him. "This will all work out, Lucas. Our marriage. The adoption."

He shook his head. "Maybe this is all wrong. What the hell do I know about children?"

She smiled. "You'll figure it all out. Every new parent has a lot to learn. And babies don't come with instruction manuals."

Dipping his head down to her, he skimmed his lips lightly across her brow. "But I have to know now. I have to do it right."

She stroked his back. "You're allowed a few mistakes, Lucas."

"Not with a child." He shook his head again and she could feel the motion ruffling her hair. "Never with a child."

Drawing back, Allie looked up at him. "No parent is perfect."

"They can be." His cheekbones stood out as his jaw tightened. "I can be."

"Lucas…" She brought her hands up to his face. "You're going to do it wrong sometimes. Every parent does. Mine did, I'm sure yours…"

The bleakness that entered his eyes shocked her. She saw pain distilled there, pain so deep it must go straight to his soul. She tried to remember what he had said about his parents, could only recall that they were both gone.

"Lucas," she said softly, fingertips grazing his hair lightly. "We both survived whatever errors our parents made. Your child will, too."

The gray of his eyes darkened, a storm raging in them. As Allie watched, a fire ignited there, burning away the pain. He pulled her closer to him, pressing her so tightly to his body she could barely breathe.

He bent his head to her, his fingers tangling in her hair, his mouth descending on hers. Her heart jolted into overdrive at the first touch of his lips, the first feel of his tongue tasting her. The passion she'd struggled against exploded like a flash fire when his tongue thrust inside her mouth.

She wanted to touch him everywhere at once, along his muscled back, down his hair-roughened arms, his throat, the angles of his face. She tugged at his shirt, pulled it free from his slacks, slipped her hands underneath to feel his warm skin. He groaned in her mouth as she skimmed her palms to his sides, then his chest, and she could feel the sound as well as hear it.

Gripping her hips he lifted her into his lap. She could feel his arousal against her hip and ached to have him inside her. He need only pull her down with him on the couch and they could have paradise.

Caught in the mindless passion, the strident voice deep inside her that had urged she keep her distance from this man had quieted. Her body had taken over, squirming against him with its own imperatives.

Suddenly, Lucas tore his mouth from her. "I'm sorry," he rasped. Hands on her waist, he slid her from his lap, sprang from the sofa. "Sorry."

Allie sat weak and breathless on the sofa. His arousal

still pushed against the fly of his khakis; the sight of it sent her mind spinning in a thousand different erotic directions.

Covering her face with her hands, she willed the images away. "We can't keep doing this, Lucas. It confuses everything, confuses...me."

"I'm sorry," he said again.

She swung her head up. "I was just as much a part of that as you were."

Hands shoved in his pockets, he turned away from her, stared out at the lake now shrouded in blackness. "Nevertheless, I damn well ought to have better self-control."

"Lucas." She rose on shaky legs. "I'm not placing blame. It's just..." Fingertips against her brow, she tried to frame the words. "I can't become sexually involved with you," she finally stated baldly. She looked up at him, to judge his reaction.

His profile could have been carved in granite for all his expression changed. "Of course not. It wasn't part of the deal."

He made it sound so cold-blooded. But how could she tell him the real reason they had to keep their distance? That if they made love, there would be nothing to hold her heart back. Even now it would take very little convincing for her to interpret the feelings she'd been harboring for him as love.

It wasn't love at all. It was only respect for his dignity and honesty, sympathy for the troubled emotions he could neither express nor completely keep inside him.

There were no words for her feelings, so she simply agreed with his assessment. "No, it wasn't part of our deal."

"I promised you a platonic relationship. I apologize for breaking that pledge." He turned toward her. "Look—I brought home work this weekend and still haven't gotten to it. I'll see you out."

His abrupt dismissal left her reeling. She nearly reminded him he'd promised her courtesy, too. But as he picked up the bowls and picked up the mugs, she could see the tremor in his hands. In that moment, he needed her gone, needed the space of his solitude.

She picked up her purse, waited for him to return from the kitchen. He didn't touch her as he handed over her car keys, then escorted her outside. Although she longed to, she resisted the urge to hug him goodbye.

In the cool darkness of the autumn night, she slipped inside her car, cranked down the window. "See you Monday, then."

He tipped his head in assent, then reached in his pocket again. "I nearly forgot." He dangled a set of keys.

Allie held out her hand and he dropped them into her palm. At her questioning look, he said, "For the house, the garage, the boathouse. I haven't had the car keys duplicated yet."

He stepped back from the car then, one hand up in a wave, the house lights behind him backlighting him into silhouette. Setting his keys on the seat beside her, she started the car.

As she pulled away, she knew he watched her. When she reached the end of the drive, just before pulling onto the street, she looked in her rearview mirror. He still stood there, a tall, lonely shadow.

Chapter Six

Soft autumn light filtered through the stained-glass windows on either side of the sanctuary, washing the floor in reds, blues and greens. Beside her sister in the vestibule, Allie peeked around the open doors.

Lucas stood at the altar, impeccable in a charcoal-gray suit. She couldn't make out his expression, couldn't see if it was calm or anxious, if the emotions roiling inside her were mirrored in him.

Sherril leaned in close and whispered in Allie's ear. "You're sure about this?"

No! a voice screamed inside of Allie. "Of course I'm sure," she said aloud.

"We could still make a run for it." Sherril tipped her head toward the exit doors, her hands resting on her swollen belly. "Although in my case it would be more like a waddle."

Allie giggled, a slightly hysterical sound. "My luck, you'd go into labor halfway through our escape."

Sherril smiled, laid her fingers lightly on Allie's bare shoulder. "Truly, you can change your mind if you want."

Her sister's earnest expression was nearly Allie's undoing. She blinked away the temptation of tears. "We're in the church, Sherril. It's a little late for cold feet."

"No." Sherril turned Allie toward her. "Allie, if there's anything…" She looked away a moment, then back at Allie, her expression troubled. "I noticed at the rehearsal dinner…he doesn't touch you, barely looks your way. Are you positive—"

"I'm positive," Allie assured her sister. How could she tell Sherril the truth, that Lucas kept his distance to avoid setting off a wildfire? "We're both sure."

Unable to meet her sister's gaze any longer, Allie turned to look up the center aisle of the church again. Lucas stood motionless, head up, shoulders pulled back, arms at his sides. Only his hands moved, alternately curling into fists, then straightening as if all his energy centered there.

Allie pulled back from the door, smoothed the pale-gray satin of her skirt, tugged at the dove-gray lace bodice of the Empire-style dress. "Is my zipper zipped?" she asked her sister. "Are my hooks hooked?"

"Yes. You're an exquisite bride," Sherril told her, touching the tendril of hair that curled by Allie's ear.

Would Lucas think so? Allie wondered as she lowered the gray tulle veil over her face. "Then I'm ready."

Sherril poked her head around the doors, nodding to

the organist. The elderly woman broke off from Pachelbel to start the wedding processional. Another touch Lucas would just as soon have eliminated. If Allie had left it up to him, there would be no music, there would be no flowers flanking the altar, and the ceremony would be just long enough to allow them each to say "I do."

At least he'd left the dress up to her, would see it for the first time today. As Sherril's seven-year-old daughter, Lisa, headed down the aisle with her basket of rose petals, followed by her five-year-old brother, Daniel, with the pillow holding the ring, Allie agonized over her choice of wedding dress. Far from traditional, the bodice rose to a standup collar and left her shoulders completely bare. The long A-line skirt had a slit up the back that ended just below her knees.

Sherril gave Allie a smile and a quick squeeze on the arm before following her son. So close to her due date, Sherril's hands holding her small bouquet rested on her belly. Her dress, borrowed from a pregnant friend, swirled in soft shades of rose and gray, a perfect match for Allie's gown.

Now the music swelled, cueing Allie. One mass of nerves, she dragged in a long breath, wishing for the hundredth time her father could be here, his hand on her arm. She'd gone as far as to call the nursing home yesterday, to see if there was any possibility of bringing him down for the ceremony. But the nurse at the care home told her French was going through a bad patch and there was no telling whether his mind would be clear enough for Allie's wedding.

So she would walk up the aisle alone. Filling her lungs one last time, she rounded the door, stepped into the aisle. Clutching her bouquet of baby's breath and pale-pink roses tied with gray ribbon, she tried to still the trembling in her hands. She kept her gaze fixed on Reverend Harmon up by the altar, too cowardly to look at Lucas yet. Ridiculous as it seemed, she craved his approval of her dress, her hair, even the gray slippers on her feet.

Sherril had reached the altar, turned to stand on the reverend's left, opposite Lucas's attorney friend, John. When Allie had met John last night at the rehearsal dinner, his warm, outgoing nature had surprised her. How such dissimilar men as he and Lucas had managed to become friends in college, Allie couldn't understand.

Now...she had to look at him now. Her crossed fingers hidden by her bouquet, she lifted her gaze to Lucas. She nearly stumbled as her heartbeat lurched into high speed. Then tears pricked her eyes.

He looked stunned, his mouth slightly open, his eyes wide, their gray so soft her heart melted. The yearning in his face, like a child whose greatest wish has just been granted, reached deep inside her. As Allie stepped up beside him, turned toward him and reached for his hand, a suspicion flared within—that there was more to this marriage than either of them might want to admit.

She shoved the thought aside, not wanting to consider the feelings that begged for recognition. It was only the ritual, the ceremony that filled her with such longing, her own wish that the vows they were about to speak could be true.

Lucas's warm hand enfolded hers. She clung to the bouquet of roses as if it were a lifeline, telling herself again and again this was only pretend. It wasn't really the beginnings of love she felt in her own heart, or adoration she foolishly persuaded herself she saw in

Lucas's eyes. It was just the music, the church, the presence of her family around her, her fervent wish her father could be here. It was the tumultuous emotions that confused her, led her to believe the impossible.

She dimly heard the words Reverend Harmon spoke, then Lucas's low quiet voice repeating the wedding vows. He said each phrase with characteristic intensity, never mind this union's built-in time limit. When it was her turn, she found herself caught up in the magic of the ritual. Her voice quavered over the final "I do," tears threatening to close her throat.

Lucas slid the wedding ring on her finger, and she gazed down at it, the concrete symbol of their promise. That the promise would only last a year or two she banished from her mind.

Then the pastor invited the groom to kiss his bride, and Lucas reached for Allie's veil. His hands trembled a little as they pulled away the gray tulle, then smoothed it behind her head. He paused a moment before he leaned in, and Allie couldn't take a breath.

As he lowered his lips to hers, Allie was starkly aware this would be the first time he had touched her since her visit to his house last week. She felt grateful for their audience, that there was something to keep their passion from flaring out of control.

He pressed his lips to hers, enough to satisfy the tradition of a kiss, not nearly enough to quench Allie's thirst. As he drew back, she had to squelch the urge to throw her arms around him and haul him back against her. Instead she turned to her sister to retrieve her bouquet, then with Lucas beside her, she faced the sparsely filled pews.

Behind her, Reverend Harmon beamed. "I now introduce to you Mr. and Mrs. Taylor."

Allie Taylor. That cemented their commitment like nothing else. When he'd asked if she would take his name, she had said yes without equivocation. It had immediately seemed right and now the magnitude of what she'd done washed over her.

At Lucas's urging, she started back down the aisle with the wedding march swelling on the organ. Pale-pink rose petals cushioned her feet with each step, but her greatest awareness centered on Lucas's hand gripping hers. When they stepped out into the autumn sunshine, rice showered them, thrown with gusto by her nieces and nephews.

She turned to face her sister and brother, their spouses and her grinning nieces and nephews. And with the suddenness of a thunderclap, she lost her tenuously balanced control and burst into tears.

Lucas stood alone in the quiet of the *Cocina Caldera* kitchen, the hum of voices drifting through the doors from the dining room beyond. He didn't like to think he was hiding, but in bald truth he was. He needed this brief space to breathe, to let the day's events settle inside him.

His suit jacket hanging on a chair in the dining room, his shirtsleeves rolled up and his tie loosened, he should have been the picture of relaxation. But although the ceremony was finished and the post-wedding celebration was winding down, every fiber of his being felt on edge.

He knew why, could spell the answer out in five letters—Allie. His new wife. The woman he'd married not for love but for convenience. And yet he couldn't shake loose the vision of her when he had first seen her at the church, moving up the aisle toward him.

Settling against the butcher-block counter beside him, he surrendered to the memory, closed his eyes and let the image come. He recalled the stuttering of his heart, the overwhelming awe of her beauty. In that instant, he'd felt like kneeling at her feet, pouring out his gratitude that she would be his wife.

His fervor had shaken him bone-deep. His response to Allie had caught him entirely off guard.

The clatter of the kitchen doors snapped his eyes open. Inez, her hands full of dirty plates, grinned at him. "Looking forward to the night to come, *guapo?*"

His stomach lurched and his groin tightened at the thought of a wedding night with Allie. He scowled at Inez as she slid the dishes into a waiting bus tray. "Just looking for a little time alone," he said pointedly.

"With your new bride?" Inez poked him in the ribs. *"¿La primera noche?"*

The first night. But there wouldn't be a first night with Allie. Not if he kept his head, upheld his solemn promise. His heart thundered in his chest, showing him just how tenuous his grip was on his libido.

He raked a hand through his hair. "Sometimes you're just too damned personal, Inez."

Her expression softened and she gave his hand a squeeze. "Hey, Lucas, I'm sorry. You never could take the teasing."

He clumsily patted her hand. "This is just a little new to me."

Her brow furrowed. "Not so new. There was Carol, remember?"

He shook his head. "Carol was..." He tried to frame the words. A thousand years ago and a million miles from the enigma of Allie. "Carol was different."

"Because you didn't love her," Teresa declared as

she carried a half-empty platter of pork *carnitas* into the kitchen. "This one you love. This one is *la esposa de tu alma.*"

His soul mate. But she wasn't; she was only his temporary wife. But he couldn't tell that to Teresa. She'd gotten so much joy from his marriage, from the chance to host this party.

There was really no point in telling her the truth. Let her believe his and Allie's union was a love match. When they parted later, Teresa would deal with it, just as she had with Carol.

So he smiled at Teresa, let her tug him down to her diminutive height so she could kiss his cheek. *"Buena suerte, mijo,"* she said.

Allie watched from the kitchen doorway as Teresa went up on tiptoes to press a kiss to Lucas's cheek. The older woman's wish for good luck Allie understood; the other word, *mijo,* was unfamiliar. The softness in Lucas's eyes as he gazed down at Teresa was just as foreign to Allie.

He straightened, spotting her in the doorway; the tenderness vanished in a heartbeat. He glanced quickly at Teresa then back at Allie as if to assess whether she'd seen the older woman's gesture. Allie doubted Lucas would feel comfortable knowing she had.

Seeing Allie, Teresa beamed, pride lighting her weathered face. As if she simply couldn't contain her joy, she enveloped Allie in a hug, then planted a kiss on her cheek. Gesturing to her daughter, Inez, she hurried out. Inez winked at Lucas as she departed, then Allie and Lucas were alone.

She approached him hesitantly. "It's after nine. I thought we ought to go, let the Calderas close up."

He checked his watch, and she saw his surprise when he registered the time. "Sorry. I didn't know it was so late."

His glower was spoiled by the red imprint of Teresa's lipstick on his cheek. "Good thing I saw Teresa kiss you." She reached up, rubbed with her fingers. The beginnings of a beard rasped under her fingertips. "Or I might be jealous."

The words came out in a breathy whisper. She couldn't seem to touch him without reacting.

Color rose in his face. Embarrassment? Or something else? "She's very demonstrative." He swiped at his cheek.

"You two seem very close." Allie grabbed a paper napkin, cleaned the bit of lipstick from her thumb. "You must be longtime friends."

He gave her a noncommittal shrug. "Let's get going."

The lightest touch on her shoulder turned her toward the double doors, the skirt of her gown swirling around her ankles. A frisson of awareness shot up her spine as he walked close behind her into the dining room. She could feel the heat of his hand hovering at the small of her back where the low-cut dress left her skin bare. Dangerous, impossible visions tumbled in her mind.

Allie shook off the images, focused instead on her family seated around the cluttered table. Sherril sat with shoes off, her feet in her husband's lap. Pete rubbed Sherril's feet while her youngest, Daniel, snuggled in the curve of her arm, leaning against her belly. Teresa cradled Stephen's infant girl, Juliana, while his wife, Anne, looked on in serene approval. Stephen's three-year-old, Patrick, chattered away at Lucas's friend, John, the one-way conversation ranging from the latest superhero craze to favorite dinosaurs to the icky stuff his baby sister did. John's attention wavered between Patrick's jet-speed talk and dark-eyed Inez's enigmatic smile.

Watching them all, a bittersweet longing filled Allie. This was what she'd always looked forward to having when she married, the sweet chaos of children and family. She should be looking forward tonight to a full life with the man beside her, to all the joys and sorrows, triumphs and failures life brought. Instead, an ending loomed in her future before she'd even started.

Allie moved around the table, leaning to kiss her sister's cheek, give Daniel's head a pat, then moving on to give her brother a hug. Behind her, Lucas murmured his goodbyes, shaking Pete's hand, then Stephen's and John's.

As they drifted toward the door, the ebullient Patrick raced across the room toward Lucas. "Are you my uncle now?"

Allie could see the fascination in Lucas's face, his avid interest in the small, pugnacious boy standing before him. Lucas smiled. "Yes, I am."

Patrick thrust his hand out for Lucas to shake. "Welcome to the family, Uncle Lucas."

Lucas seemed stunned, then to Allie's surprise, he went down on one knee to meet Patrick eye-to-eye. "Thank you," he said, shaking the boy's hand.

When Patrick flung his arms around his new uncle, Lucas hesitated only an instant before hugging the boy back. Then Patrick broke away, dancing back to his mother.

With his gaze still on Patrick, Lucas rose to his feet,

groped for Allie's hand. One last nod to her family and he led her from the restaurant and into the cool autumn night.

Lucas pulled up the drive to his house, acutely aware of Allie seated beside him in the Mercedes. He'd navigated the short distance from Fair Oaks to Granite Bay on automatic, his senses too full of Allie—her scent, the soft curves of her body—to even think. Now, as he stopped at the garage and clicked the door open, images crowded his mind of her in his arms, melting against him as he kissed her, touched her.

Gripping the wheel, he guided the Mercedes into the garage and cut the engine. This was a moment he'd both dreaded and anticipated—bringing Allie home as his wife. Even knowing the limits of their marriage, he couldn't seem to drive from his mind the forbidden possibilities.

She sighed, a tantalizing sound. Huddled in the suit jacket he'd given her against the chill autumn air, she rested her head against the seat, her eyes closed. Her upswept hair had come loose on the sides and the temptation to stroke it back behind her ears overpowered him.

But he didn't touch her. He opened the car door and the dome light illuminated her face. "Tired?" he asked.

She groaned. "I could sleep a week."

He jiggled the car keys in his hand. "You could still take the time off."

She turned toward him, looking up at him. "What about you?"

He shook his head. "I can't. There's the Golden Snack deal, and the fiscal year-end reports."

Her gaze was fixed on him, her direct green eyes mesmerizing. "Then I can't, either. I'd rather be..."

With you, his mind finished for her. *I'd rather be with you.*

She turned away. "I'd rather be at the office."

Of course. She wouldn't want to neglect her work. "Good. Just as well. Not the best time to take off."

He slid from the car, rounding it to open her door, take her hand and help her from the car. His jacket slid from one shoulder and when he grabbed it to pull it back into place, his wrist grazed her bare back.

Hot sensation shot straight to his core. He backed away to put space between them. "Allie."

Already moving toward the door leading to the house, she turned to him, exhaustion lining her face. He ought to leave this until tomorrow, but her tiredness would work in his favor. She had less energy to argue.

He gestured her over to the rose-gray Volvo parked between the Mercedes and his Explorer. Opening the door, he picked up the set of keys on the front seat, dangled them out to her.

"What is this?" she asked.

He pulled her hand toward him, pressed the keys into it. "Your new car."

Her eyes narrowed on him. "I have a car. My Buick."

"I had it towed to a wrecking yard earlier today."

Her mouth dropped open. The jacket slipped from her shoulder again as she straightened. "You did what?"

"Had it towed." He tried to reach for her, to pull the jacket up, but she jerked away from him.

"How could you?" Her hand closed in a fist around the keys. "That was my car."

"For God's sake, Allie, it was a death trap."

"It was my car," she repeated, her voice trembling. She stood silent a moment, eyes brimming with tears, then she threw the keys to the ground. "Damn you, Lucas Taylor."

Before he could take another breath, she was gone, and the slamming of the door to the house rang in his ears. His jacket lay crumpled in front of the Mercedes where it had fallen from her shoulders. The keys to the Volvo had landed under the car; he had to fish for them to retrieve them.

Keys biting into his hand, Lucas sank into the driver's seat of the Volvo, the plush leather upholstery giving under his weight. Good God, how could such a simple thing go so wrong?

He'd only wanted her to be safe, to have a reliable car to drive. He'd suspected she'd object to him giving it to her, which was why he'd disposed of her Buick without her knowing. Presented with a fait accompli, he'd thought she would accept the gift more willingly.

Yet he'd only managed to bring her to tears—for a second time today. The first, after the wedding ceremony, had seemed more than the usual high emotions of a new bride. He'd apparently let her down there. Somehow, in the course of the ritual, she'd needed something, asked him for it. But he hadn't even the slightest clue what she wanted him to give her.

So he gave her a damn car instead. No wonder she'd run into the house sobbing. He'd demonstrated for probably the hundredth time that he lacked what it took to be a husband. More than ready to be her lover— even now his body clamored for release in her sweetness—he hadn't the first notion how to be her beloved.

That hadn't been part of the deal, but still the real-

ization burned in the pit of his stomach like bile. He'd
failed again at making Allie happy. He would no doubt
fail as well in doing right by a child. What the hell did
he think he was doing, marrying her?

Heart heavy, his feet leaden, he locked up the Volvo
and followed Allie into the house.

Chapter Seven

After that inauspicious start, Allie's life with Lucas settled into a deceptive equanimity. They rode into work together, performed their routine tasks as they had before the marriage, drove back home together at the end of the day. They shared the meal Mrs. Vasquez had prepared for them, discussing the details of the day as if they were business partners who happened to be cohabiting.

But in Allie there was always the breathless anticipation of waiting for the other shoe to fall. Lucas never touched her in those first two weeks of their marriage, other than to take her hand to help her in and out of the car. He never said a word that could be construed as even remotely intimate, not at work, not at home. In fact, other than the short drive to work and home and the hour or so they spent at dinner, she was rarely in his company.

She might have thought the marriage would work exactly as they had planned if it weren't for those moments she caught him looking at her.

Sometimes it would happen in a meeting, when she sat with him in a room crowded with people. She would glance up at him from her laptop, see his gaze fixed on her, the heat of it searing her from head to toe. Or at the dinner table, as she raised a forkful of some rich dessert left for them by Mrs. Vasquez, the hunger in his gray eyes would consume her. It would be all she could do not to answer that hunger, not to step around the table to his side, let him pull her into his arms.

Even now, as she sat here in the sun-washed breakfast nook, her bagel uneaten on her plate, she waited for his scorching hot glance. Despite the peril of letting those feelings flash between them, she'd become addicted to the sensual rush.

He didn't disappoint her. As he lifted his coffee, he passed his gaze over her, as palpable as a touch. Allie could feel the heat rise in her cheeks, her breath becoming shorter. A tingle started up her spine and she imagined it was his fingertips, drawing a line of sensation over the length of her back.

He slammed down the mug, sloshing coffee, then sprang to his feet. Covering the short distance to the kitchen in three long strides, he grabbed a towel and dried his hand. Then with the kitchen island between them, he turned to her.

"I have to drive down to Modesto this afternoon," he said, tossing aside the towel. "I won't be back until late this evening."

Allie had sat in on enough conference calls to know TaylorMade's problems with the Modesto plant had gotten worse the last two weeks, despite Lucas's best efforts. "Did you need me with you?"

She hadn't intended to, but her tone colored the question differently, more personally—*Lucas, do you need me?* Despite her better sense, she held her breath waiting for an answer.

His palms were planted on the kitchen island. She saw something flicker in his face and wondered if he'd heard her unvoiced plea. Then he pushed away from the island, retrieved the towel from the kitchen counter.

"No." He rubbed at his hands again, as if he hadn't done a thorough enough job before. "I need you more in the office. Might need some reports, documents faxed down to Modesto."

"Fine." Allie rose from the table, took her plate and dumped the bagel and cream cheese into the trash. "We'd better get going, then."

The towel twisted in his hands. "We can't drive in together. I won't be able to bring you home."

Of course. That was what he'd been leading up to. She'd have to drive in alone in the Volvo.

Her stomach tightened in rebellion. She hadn't so much as sat in the car in the time since their wedding. Anger still nipped at her that he'd high-handedly sold her Buick out from under her.

But it couldn't be helped. She'd have to drive the car, accept the gift. She lifted her gaze to his. "Where are the keys?"

He reached into his pocket, brought them out. He placed them into her outstretched hand.

Dropping the keys into her skirt pocket, Allie moved to the dishwasher, slid her plate inside. "Thank you."

"Allie."

She hesitated before turning toward him. "Yes?"

"I'm sorry." He looked away, his gaze raking the ceiling before returning to her face. "It seems I'm always apologizing for something with you."

He said it without rancor, obviously blaming himself rather than her. A sudden insight burst inside her. As often as she compared Lucas's arrogance to her father's, this was one stark difference—unlike her father, Lucas admitted when he was wrong. Even when it was the hardest thing in the world for him to do.

Conflicting emotions swirled inside Allie—empathy for this powerful man sometimes laid low by his mistakes, and her lingering anger over his actions. "You should have asked me first about the car."

"I know. But I only wanted you to be safe."

How could she fault him for that? Allie's heart melted, washing away her ire. "Thank you."

He raised a brow in query. "For…?"

"For the car. For the apology."

He looked away again, then nodded brusquely. "You're welcome."

"Lucas…" She waited until he'd turned back to her. "I'll miss you…riding into work, I mean. And home."

He rounded the kitchen island, closed the distance between them. "I'll miss you, too." Bending, he brushed a kiss across her forehead, then tucked a strand of hair behind her ear.

The ever-present desire flared in his gray eyes, setting Allie's heart to racing. He swallowed, the movement of his strong throat entrancing.

He backed away, banging his elbow on the kitchen counter. He snatched up his briefcase, headed for the door to the garage. "See you in the office."

Over the rumble of the garage door opening, Allie heard Mrs. Vasquez calling out a hello as she came in the front door. Dazed, Allie leaned against the granite-topped island as Mrs. Vasquez entered the kitchen.

"Has Mr. Taylor gone to work?" Mrs. Vasquez asked, pulling an apron from a drawer.

"Yes. And I should, too." Waving a sketchy goodbye to the housekeeper, Allie picked up her purse and headed out to the garage. Climbing into the Volvo, she ran her hand over the butter-soft leather seat. The door shut with a satisfying, solid ka-chunk. The engine started with a quiet purr.

One hand on the leather-covered steering wheel, she reached for the gearshift, ready to shift into reverse. Her gaze fell on the center of the wheel, near the button for the horn. Attached there was an engraved gold plate, glimmering in the dim light of the garage.

Allie skimmed her fingers over the letters—Alison Taylor—and shook her head in disbelief. Each time she discovered a new depth to Lucas, another layer presented itself. Would she ever truly understand the man she'd married?

A bittersweet smile curving her lips, she backed from the garage and headed off to work.

Lucas drove north on Highway 99, his eyes hooded against the glare of the Mercedes's headlights. Exhaustion lay heavily on his shoulders. A quick glance at the car's clock—it was well past ten—and he felt even more tired. He should be home by now, sitting with Allie and watching the evening news while she read her book. Or better yet, wrapped in her arms in his bed.

No profit in letting his thoughts run in that direction. Flipping on the car fan to vent cool air on his face, he changed to the right-hand lane in anticipation of taking the Highway 50 exit. Wisps of tule fog drifted across his path as he drove, a distraction that tightened the point of tension between his eyes. Every fiber of him ached to be home, to be sharing the company of a woman he'd become frighteningly dependent upon within such a short time.

Throughout the afternoon and early evening, she'd been almost a lifeline for him. Every call he'd made to the home office had been on the pretext of business. He needed a fax of last month's sales data broken down by product category, a memo dictated over the phone then e-mailed to him, the phone number of a supplier back east. But as the day wore on, Lucas realized simply talking to Allie, just hearing her voice on the phone was a balm to his jangled nerves. She energized him, restored him.

He'd called her as he was leaving the Modesto plant, this time at home. Her voice had sounded a little sleepy and he wondered if she'd dozed off on the living-room sofa while she read. She'd had dinner without him— some of Mrs. Vasquez's chicken adobo. He'd had two calls, one from John, one from Melissa—a woman he'd dated only a few months ago—who'd been shocked to learn he was married.

Allie had promised she'd wait up for him. That was what pulled him now, weighted his foot on the accelerator, pushed his speed slightly past the limit. The quicker he got home, the sooner he could be with her. It ought to terrify him that seeing Allie meant so much to him; in fact it did. He didn't care.

As he pulled up his driveway, headlights cutting through the misty darkness, he exhaled a long breath, eager for his first glimpse of Allie. In the garage, he cut the Benz's engine, left his briefcase on the seat as he climbed from the car. Slipping into the house, he tossed his keys to the breakfast table and headed for the living room.

When he first saw her, his heart squeezed so tight in his chest he couldn't breathe. She was curled up on the sofa, sound asleep. The one lit lamp in the room cast a golden glow on her face. Her head rested on the sofa's arm, her fingers lay lax on the book she'd been reading. The softness of her parted lips, the slope of her breast under her turtleneck sweater teased him, tempted him to touch her.

He sank down on one knee beside her, brushed her dark hair from her face with the lightest of contact. "Allie," he murmured. "Allie, honey."

Her eyes fluttered open, confusion in their green depths. "Oh." The sound whispered from her lips. "I guess I fell asleep."

He couldn't help but smile. "I guess you did." His fingers were still tangled in her hair. "I'm sorry I'm so late."

She pushed herself up, and he let his hand fall back to his side. "I'm sorry you had to stay so long. Did you solve that problem with the supplier?"

He straightened, then sank onto the sofa beside her. "For now." He leaned back with a sigh. He was home now, with Allie. He could let go of the day's stress.

"You must be dead tired." She rubbed a hand down his arm, the light pressure of her fingers warming him even through his suit jacket. "Let me rub your shoulders."

Even as a tingle of sensation marched up his spine at the suggestion, his good sense sent out a warning. Having Allie's hands on him would only lead them both into perilous territory.

He looked at her sidelong. ''That's not a good idea, Allie.''

A series of emotions flickered across her face—first hurt that he'd rejected her invitation, then realization when she'd understood his meaning, then determination. ''I'm only offering to rub your shoulders, Lucas. We'll both be keeping our clothes on.''

Color rose in her cheeks, far too enticing. He should tell her no, should head off to bed, to the safety of his room. Instead he presented his back to her.

She rested her hands on his shoulders. ''You have to take off your jacket.''

He hesitated, then tugged his arms free, tossed the jacket to the other end of the sofa. Sitting stiffly, he waited for her to touch him.

His breath caught at the first gentle contact, then whooshed out as she stroked along his shoulder blades. Warmed by her palms, his skin heated beneath the thin cotton of his dress shirt. His body reacted to her nearness, sensation shooting up his spine with each pass of her hands across his back.

If she'd intended to relax him, she was failing miserably. But where the tension of the day's catastrophes had exhausted and demoralized him, Allie's touch recharged him, filled him with an urgency to act. That the act his body suggested to him was forbidden didn't seem to dampen its enthusiasm.

She dug her thumbs into the taut muscles of his neck, then along his shoulders. In the wake of the steady pressure, aches he hadn't known he'd locked in his body eased. The troubles of the day dispersed like valley mist chased by morning sun. All the yearning he'd felt driving home to Allie crystallized in that moment into pure contentment.

But his balance on that razor-sharp edge between pleasure and despair was too precarious to trust. He tried to hold back the feelings, the unfamiliar emotions. But they seemed to rush willy-nilly inside him, filling him with confusion.

Allie's gentle strokes moved slightly lower on his back to his trapezius. Suddenly realizing where her hands were moving, Lucas tensed, ready to pull away. But her sure fingers found the ugly ridge of scarring before he could shift away from her.

As she ran her fingertips along the periphery of the marred skin, Lucas grew still, frozen by anticipation of her questions. When her hands stuttered in their discovery of the expanse of ruin, from six inches below his shoulder to just above his waist, a sick dread built in his gut. He guessed at the horror she must feel, the aversion.

Then her hands moved again, gliding up his back. He felt her lean close, felt her lips press to the nape of his neck. In that moment, he thought his heart might burst.

"Better?" she murmured.

He wanted to reach behind him for her, to curve his arms around her and pull her close. He kept his hands in his lap. "Much better. Thank you."

She rested her cheek against his back. "Shall we turn on the news? The eleven o'clock should still be on."

He ached to say yes, to spend an hour, two, so close to her. But the roil of emotions in him drove him to his feet. He felt the coolness of the air between them when they parted.

"I'm pretty beat." Reaching for his jacket, he slung it over his shoulder. "I'm heading for bed."

Can I join you? he imagined her saying. *Can I sleep with you tonight?*

But of course she said nothing of the kind. She just smiled, her expression sweet and wistful all at once. "See you in the morning, then." She reached for her book. "I'm going to read a bit more, then I'll be up."

He nodded good-night, started for the stairs. He thought he could feel her gaze on him, but he didn't dare look back. If he did, he might not be able to leave her.

He felt so edgy, he thought he'd never fall asleep. But his brutal exhaustion took him nearly the moment his head hit the pillow.

Allie set aside her book and rubbed at her burning eyes. It was nearly 2:00 a.m., long past time she went to bed. The book wasn't that riveting—she just felt too restless to sleep.

She sighed, gazing up the stairs Lucas had climbed hours ago. It hadn't felt right today having him gone, even though he was only seventy miles away in Modesto. Each time she'd passed his empty office, a hollow ache had settled in her stomach. She'd found herself staring at the phone, waiting for it to ring, willing it to be him on the other end of the line.

Each time he'd called, for a quarterly fiscal report or a list of employee salaries, her heart had beat faster. When he'd call back to confirm he'd received the data, the rumble of his voice in her ear sent her pulse racing.

When she'd phoned him at six to let him know she was leaving for the day, he'd sounded harried and frustrated. She wanted nothing more than to be there with him, to soothe him.

Glancing at the clock, she winced at the late hour.

She ought to at least take the book upstairs and read in bed. Snapping off the light, she headed for the stairs. When she reached the second-floor landing, she looked toward Lucas's room, wishing the light still burned under the closed door, that she could go inside and spend a few more minutes with him.

In her room, she quickly went through her nightly routine of face washing and teeth brushing, then threw on an oversized T-shirt for bed. Although it hung nearly to her knees, the sleep shirt wouldn't be warm enough when winter settled in with its chill rain. But for now, the short-sleeved shirt was sufficient for cool autumn nights.

Reaching for the covers, she realized she'd left the book downstairs. She debated with herself whether she should even bother retrieving it—she had few enough hours until morning. But reading a couple more pages would help relax her.

She got as far as the landing when she heard a long, low groan from Lucas's room. She moved closer to the door, pressed her ear against it. Another cry, half scream, half moan, filtered through the heavy wooden door.

"Lucas?" She said his name softly at first, loathe to wake him. "Lucas?"

"No!" His shout sent a chill arrowing up her spine. *"No!"*

She hesitated only another heartbeat before wrenching open the door. The light from the landing spilled into the room, dimly illuminating the large bed that dominated the far wall. Lucas lay tangled in the covers, writhing and struggling against some unknown demon.

"Please!" His pleading tone gripped her heart. "Please... No!"

She quickly covered the distance to the bed, sank to the edge. "Lucas."

His arm shot out, his hand grabbing a fistful of her T-shirt. "Please," he pleaded again, his eyes still shut tight. He tugged at her.

Murmuring his name, Allie stroked his bare arm, from wrist to shoulder. His hand went lax, releasing her shirt, then his arm slipped around her. He pulled her toward him, shifting his body until she lay beside him.

A thin blanket and sheet provided the only barrier between them. With the covers low on his hips, Lucas held Allie tight against the bare expanse of his chest. The soft curls there tickled her cheek, tempted her to touch them. Tentatively she placed her hand on the taut muscle, threaded her fingers into the nest of hair.

He sighed, the long exhalation signaling the dispersal of his nightmare. Bringing his other arm around her, he pulled her even closer so she had to hook her leg over his. As his heat seeped into her, warming her despite the lack of covers, a sense of well-being permeated every cell of her being.

As her hand moved in a lazy, slowing pattern along his side, his back, sleep lapped at her, tugging her closer to unconsciousness. When her fingers brushed again against the scar she'd felt earlier on his back, he stirred, seemed to nearly wake. As she stroked lightly, he drifted back into sleep and only a few moments later, she followed.

Before she even opened her eyes, bliss infused Allie when she woke the next morning. Lucas still held her close, one arm cushioning her head, the other draped over her waist. Her T-shirt had ridden up to her hips and she'd flung one leg over his. The covers lay rumpled on the other side of the bed. There was nothing between her and his rigid manhood but the thin knit of her panties.

He thrust against her and her eyes flew open. From the laxness of his face, she realized he wasn't yet awake, aware of what he was doing. Even so, with his arousal pressed against her, her breath caught and wet warmth spread between her legs.

She had to wake him, to stop him. But the enervating pleasure of the pressure against her sensitive center kept her mute. Even as her cheeks flamed with the shame of her enjoyment of his unconscious state, she shut her eyes, wriggled closer to him.

She knew the instant he woke. He stilled, his manhood still thrust against her. His low groan vibrated against her, heightening the sensations his body sent through her. Forcing herself to open her eyes, she met his gaze.

The harsh lines of his face, so relaxed in sleep, stood out sharply in the pale morning light. "Allie?"

She started to pull away, but he stopped her. "I…you…" she stuttered. "You had a nightmare. I just…"

He stroked her hair back from her brow. "You came to comfort me." His voice was as harsh as his face although he didn't seem angry.

Allie tried a smile. "You didn't seem to want to let me go."

"No," he said quietly. "I don't."

She puzzled over his statement, over his enigmatic expression. "Do you remember it? The nightmare?"

His jaw tightened. "I don't remember my dreams."

He wasn't being honest with her; she could see it in

his eyes. As she slid a hand up his back, her fingertips skimmed the edges of his scar. He flinched, sucking in a breath.

Allie jerked her hand away. "I'm sorry. Does it hurt?"

He shook his head slowly, but Allie saw pain reflected in his face, mingled with a soul-deep grief. In that moment she would have done anything to ease the agony within him.

"Lucas—"

He lowered his mouth to hers, covered her body with his own. While his tongue thrust between her lips, the heated length of his manhood burned her thighs.

"Lucas..." she moaned, trembling, as passion sapped everything from her body but need.

Chapter Eight

If he had taken her in that moment she would have let him.

So overwhelmed with sensation was she, every fiber of her being screamed for release. But when she might have expected him to rip her shirt, her panties from her, he seemed to gather his control back around him. His kiss gentled, his lips skimming across hers, his tongue trailing along her cheek and jaw, flicking lightly in her ear.

Rearing up over her, he cradled her face in his hands. "We can stop now, Allie," he said, his voice rough-edged.

His eyes were hooded as he gazed down at her, something hiding in the gray depths, a puzzle that teased her to untangle it.

Even as he dragged in ragged breath after ragged breath, he kept those few inches of distance from her.

The taut muscles of his shoulders stood out in ropy tension.

An ache started in her chest, the longing to soothe him, to be his balm against the devils raging inside him an undeniable urgency. Even more than the sexual need that flared inside her, echoed in his gray eyes, the yearning to comfort him drove her. Surely in intimacy, in a joining of their bodies, the walls would come down and Lucas, the real man, vulnerable and powerful all at once, would step clear of his self-imposed chains.

As answer, Allie curved a hand behind his head, tugging him closer. "Love me," she whispered as she touched her lips to his.

He resisted a moment more, pulling back. "I haven't got protection," he said harshly.

Protection. She hadn't even considered it, rejoiced now when she realized she was in the least fertile part of her cycle. "Don't worry," she murmured. "It's a safe time for me."

She could feel him tremble as if he warred with the urging of his passion. When he reached for her again, he guided his hand leisurely down her body, along her collarbone to her shoulder, down her arm. Allie shivered in reaction to his featherlight touch as he caressed the pulse point on her wrist, moved back up to rub his thumb across the crook of her elbow.

He slid his palm across her ribcage, between her breasts, fingers skidding close to the soft mound. Circling one breast with the heel of his hand, he kept his gaze fixed on her face as if to measure her response. Impatient with the T-shirt between them, Allie reached for the hem, intending to strip it off. But he caught her hand, hooked it back behind his head.

She wanted to scream at him that he was going too

slowly, but then fingertips grazed her sensitive nipple and the sound that spilled from her throat was a long, low moan. Flicking at her nipple with his thumb, he watched her, seeming to drink in her passion. Then he lowered his head and pulled her nipple into his mouth.

His hand had moved to her other breast and while his fingers teased and tortured there, he grazed her nipple with his teeth through the wet knit of the T-shirt. Sensation shot from the hard buds of her breast to her core, pooling between her thighs and driving another moan from her. Her restless legs tangled with his, then she drew them up, letting him settle between them. She tightened her thighs around his hips, pivoting her pelvis forward until she could feel him intimately pressing at the V of her legs.

He rasped in a breath, his lips and hands still for a moment. His eyes squeezed shut, tension centered in his jaw, in the throbbing pulse at his throat. Another shaky breath, then he reached unhurriedly for her shirt, kissing and stroking as he pulled it up then off her. He kissed each breast, then moved lower, fingers hooking in her panties. He waited for her to lift her hips, then he drew them from her body.

He sat back on his heels, his gaze burning into her, his arousal begging for her touch. She reached for him, curving her hands around the hard flesh, stroking along its length. He threw back his head, hands fisted, a groan dragged from him.

Then he grabbed her wrists, pulled her hands away, anchoring them above her head. Arching his body over hers, he kissed her throat, his lips moving softly down, between her breasts, along the line of her ribcage. Her breath caught as her skin rippled in response.

Releasing her hands, he glided his fingertips along

her arms, dipping in lightly at her throat, then following the trail of his lips between her breasts. His mouth moved lower, his tongue flicking at her navel, then her hipbones on either side. His hands gripped her hips as his lips continued their moist path lower, to the juncture of her thighs, to the soft curls there.

When his tongue dipped into the cleft of her thighs, her eyes flew open as her hips arched from the bed. His hands tightened on her, holding her in place as his intimate kiss continued. He splayed his hands, thumbs reaching to part her soft folds, tongue stroking her center, bringing her wave after wave of pleasure.

She groped for him, fingers threading through his hair. She couldn't lie still. With her hips held in place, her legs thrashed on the bed as tension built between her thighs. Frantic with sensation, she locked her gaze with his, saw triumph burning in his gray eyes.

When she thought she would die of the pleasure, he thrust his fingers inside her and sent her rocketing into ecstasy. Her body seemed to explode. Her fingers went lax in his hair, her arms slipping nerveless to the bed.

Before she could recover, Lucas rose up to cover her body. With one swift thrust he entered her, filling her. Immediately another climax flooded her, clenching her muscles around him, driving a moan from her throat. His face buried in her neck, Lucas thrust into her, again and again, until she spasmed into another incredible peak.

She knew the instant he joined her in paradise, could feel his entire body go rigid in reaction. Her entire world centered in that moment on the joining of their bodies, the intimate link between them. Her heart leapt in sheer joy, struggling to bring to life emotions she'd fought to keep at bay. Emotions she refused to think about just now as the aftermath of their lovemaking lapped at her, bringing her back down.

Her thighs still clutched his hips, holding him tight. She relaxed them, still keeping him cradled between them. Her hands drifted across his back, grazing his scar with the lightest touch.

She waited for him to lift his head, to show her his soul through his eyes. Because surely they'd battered down the barriers between them at last, setting them both on a new path. She had only to see his eyes to be certain.

But rather than raise his head, he levered himself from her, eased from between her thighs. When she thought he would stretch out beside her and take her into his arms, he turned away, seating himself on the far edge of the wide bed. He kept his back to her as the chill morning air bit into her flesh.

In the dim light filtering through the shut plantation shutters, the scar across his back was only a shade darker than the rest of his skin. Even still, Allie's heart sank at the extent of the mark, from just below his shoulder to nearly his waist in a roughly triangular shape. She wanted to move her hand over it, to wipe away the memories, wipe away the pain. But when she reached over to touch him lightly at the base of his spine, he flinched away from the contact. Rising to his feet, he moved to the shutters, opened them slightly to gaze out at the burgeoning day.

Allie sat up, clutching the sheet over her breasts. "Lucas."

"We'd better get ready for work." His voice sounded dead. "I've got a meeting first thing."

Stunned, Allie scrambled for something to say, to

bring back the intimacy. "Lucas, we should...shouldn't we talk?"

His shoulders tightened briefly. "About what, Allie?"

Allie felt suddenly sick. He wouldn't acknowledge what they'd just done, the incredible passion they'd shared. She watched with uneasy fascination as his left hand squeezed into a fist. Their intimacy had done nothing to strip away Lucas's barriers; in fact it had rebuilt them, stronger than ever.

Tears gathered in her eyes and she shook in her effort to suppress them. "I'll go get dressed," she gasped out, hurriedly grabbing up her T-shirt, throwing it over her head. She had no idea where her panties had gotten to, didn't want to take the time to look for them. She nearly ran from the room and back to the sanctuary of her own.

She slammed the door shut, pressing her back against it as if to hold the emotions at bay. But they took hold of her anyway, taking the strength from her legs so that she collapsed to the floor. Her sobs sounded loud and ugly in the room and she feared Lucas would hear her. But when he didn't come to check on her, she cried even harder with the realization that if he had heard her, he didn't care enough to see if she was all right.

He didn't care, he *couldn't* care. He'd locked his heart so tightly against the pain of his past, a hurt he refused to share with her, he might never learn to care. He would certainly never learn to love.

Allie buried her face in her hands, felt the tears slipping between her fingers. Heaven help her, she was already three-quarters in love with him. Their lovemaking had tipped her precariously close to a precipice she ought to never have approached. Because once she made that leap, once she gave her heart completely, she had no hope of surviving the jagged rocks of Lucas's indifference.

After that morning, Allie had ample time alone to nurse her wounded heart. Lucas suddenly found it necessary to tour all of TaylorMade's manufacturing plants, to judge their efficiency and issues of worker safety. Although in the past he might have taken Allie with him to assist, there was no question of that now. He left her at home and Allie ached at being pushed aside that way.

Each day she sat at her desk, his open empty office looming behind her, her work a blur of numbers and meaningless words as she created spreadsheets and typed documents. Lucas called seldom, as if he could bear only a minimal amount of contact with her.

Now, as she negotiated the curves of Interstate 80 on her way to her Sunday visit with her father, Allie again recalled her most recent conversation with Lucas. He'd phoned late on Friday, asking for status on several pending projects. She'd hung onto every clipped word, tried to draw out the conversation as long as possible. Then, just before he said goodbye, he announced he'd be staying in Chicago at least until Tuesday. She thought her heart would break from loneliness.

She passed the Reno city limits sign and started watching for the exit for her father's care home. Although she tried to hold them at bay, images of her lovemaking with Lucas tormented her. If only she hadn't gone to Lucas's room to comfort him, if only she hadn't touched him, if only she hadn't lain down beside him late into the night.

She should never have questioned him, never have let him kiss her, should have escaped from his bed the moment passion had flared between them. She agonized over every separate act, over each step she'd taken until it had been too late to turn back.

If only. A useless, useless sentiment. Her real mistake had been in thinking that making love with Lucas would make a difference, that it would bring them closer. She had only herself to blame for the heartache that never seemed to ease.

Allie pulled into the parking lot of the care home, found an empty space next to her sister's car. Rather than all the family members visiting French at once, they tried to space out their time with him. On a bad day, too many people all at once agitated and frightened French, when he couldn't remember their faces. On a good day, their separate visits were a pleasant diversion, stretching out his enjoyment of their company.

Allie reached her father's room, then hesitated in the doorway. With a glance she took in her sister's tense face, her father's scowl as he sat in an orange plastic chair by the window. Her heart sank. Today would not be a good day.

Sherril gave Allie a quick smile that was nearly a grimace, then bent to kiss the old man goodbye. French ducked away, scooting his chair back out of her reach.

With a sigh, Sherril touched her father lightly on the shoulder. "See you later, Dad." She gave Allie a quick hug as she passed. "Good luck," she whispered.

On top of everything else, Allie wasn't sure she could bear an awkward, combative visit with her father.

She was half-tempted to turn around and leave, certain French wouldn't even notice her absence. But when she looked at the lonely old man hunched in the chair by the window, she knew she couldn't bear to leave him alone.

"Hi, Dad," she called out as she eased into the room. "It's me, Allie."

He didn't look at her, didn't even acknowledge that he'd heard her. Familiar tears pricked at Allie's eyes, tightened her throat. They'd lived with this cruel illness for nearly two years, but fresh grief always overwhelmed her when she first saw him.

She grabbed the other chair in the room and slid it over close to him. Seating herself carefully, she avoided contact. "How are you, Dad?"

For another long moment, he stared out the window as if she didn't exist. Then slowly, he turned to face her. "Elizabeth?"

An ache twisted Allie's heart. "No, it's Allie, your daughter."

French put his frail hands on her shoulders. "Elizabeth, is that you?"

Allie was about to correct him again when his eyes lit with an incredible joy. "Elizabeth! You're here!" He smiled, a gesture he'd nearly abandoned in the last few months. Love shone in his face.

How could she destroy the illusion his ravaged mind saw? She forced a smile. "Yes, I'm here."

He drew her into his arms, hugged her tightly. "They told me you died. But I knew you couldn't have. I knew you wouldn't leave me."

Tears filled Allie's eyes, wet her cheeks. She drew back as her father let her go, tried to swipe away the tears before French saw them.

But she wasn't quick enough. "What's wrong, Elizabeth? Is it the kids? Are they okay?"

Allie gave his shoulder a little squeeze. "Fine, everyone's fine."

"Is it Allie?" He laughed, a dry, rusty sound. "Don't you worry about her, Elizabeth. She might be as headstrong as her old man, but she's a good girl." He beamed, pride lighting his face. "She'll do fine."

For a moment, Allie could scarcely breathe. Her father, French Dickenson, proud of her? An unexpected joy bubbled up inside her. "Allie's fine, Dad. She's just fine."

At her quiet words, French stared intently at her as if trying hard to figure something out. "I've been sick," he said slowly. He peered at her a long time. "Allie? When did you get here?"

Allie swallowed back the threat of fresh tears. "Just now. How are you doing, Dad?"

He slumped in his chair, rubbed at his face. "Tired…so tired." He reached for her hand. "Help me to bed. I need a nap."

She supported him with an arm around his waist, her stomach churning at his slight weight. Once he was settled under the covers, she sat back down and waited until he fell asleep. She stayed a long while, watching his thin chest rise and fall, her throat constricted with the effort not to cry.

She kept her tears in check as she drove home, as she walked into the quiet, lonely house aching for Lucas. With all her heart she wished she had him to hold right now, had him to comfort her. But he might as well be on the moon as in Chicago, so distant was he from her. Distant and no way to bring him close.

When she passed his bedroom door, she couldn't

resist the pull of his wide, neatly made bed. She stepped inside the room, kicked off her shoes, then undressed in a daze, leaving her slacks and blouse in an untidy pile on the floor. In bra and panties, she climbed beneath the thick comforter.

If she couldn't have Lucas, she would have this pale substitute—the soft pillows, the warm covers still imbued with his scent. With a sigh, she nestled in the bed and let sleep take her, bringing her dreams of Lucas.

An interminable three weeks passed without Lucas and Allie thought she would go mad. When he called the office early Monday morning to inform her he intended to spend at least another week in New Jersey exploring a possible merger opportunity, it took everything in her not to shout at him in her frustration. But what could she say? I want you here with me? Please come home, I need you? That would only drive him further away.

Instead, she dutifully took down the contact information he gave her and arranged for two of his vice presidents to continue filling in for him. She considered heading back home, taking the rest of the day off. The stress had begun to wear on her so much she'd been sick to her stomach the last few days. But curling up in Lucas's bed listening to the quiet of the empty house just seemed too lonely.

When the phone rang again, every nerve in Allie's body stood at attention in hopes it was Lucas calling back. Her heart fell when the man at the other end of the line asked if Lucas was in. Allie recognized the voice; she'd taken enough messages from Lucas's attorney friend, John, to know him when he called.

She took a breath to calm herself, to erase the disappointment from her tone. "Sorry, John, he's in New Jersey this week. I can give you the number of his hotel."

"Yeah, sure—no, on second thought, you can tell him as well as me." He laughed self-consciously. "Can't quite get used to him having a wife."

Allie pinched the bridge of her nose, driving off the ever-ready tears. "It's still new for us, too."

"Just let him know, next time you talk to him, I can set up a home visit any time."

"I guess he'd have to be home for that, wouldn't he?" She sucked in a breath, wishing she could suck back in the bitter words as easily. "Sorry. Things aren't much fun around here when he's gone." Praying John would assume her irritation arose from the extra work-load with the boss gone, Allie waited through the extended silence.

"Is everything going okay with you two?" he asked finally.

Her lower lip stung from the pressure of her teeth. "Fine. We're fine."

"Allie…" John paused. "I probably know Lucas better than anyone. If you wanted to talk…"

The sympathy in his voice tipped her over the edge. Knowing he couldn't help but hear the tears in her voice, Allie struggled to get the words out. "Are you free for lunch?"

"Absolutely," he said without hesitation. "Give me a place and time and I'll be there."

So shaken, she could barely think, she stuttered, "*Cocina Caldera?* Is noon okay?"

"Perfect. I'll see you there."

After hanging up, she rose from her desk and went into Lucas's office where she knew she'd have some

privacy. She wiped away her tears, blew her nose and
downed a drink of water from the cooler. In all the
roaring fights she'd had over the years with her father,
he'd never brought her to tears. A month and a half
married to Lucas and she seemed to cry every day.

She'd had enough. She was tired of moping around,
letting her aching heart rule her day. Determined to
ferret out some answers from John at lunch, Allie
swiped at her face with a tissue one last time and strode
back to her desk. The rest of the morning she spent
buried in work, holding thoughts of Lucas at bay. But
he always hovered there, never quite out of sight.

Seated at a table near the door, Allie saw John enter
Cocina Caldera and look around him. His gaze
skimmed right over Allie, lighting on Inez as she
moved gracefully through the restaurant with her arms
full of plates piled high with food. When Inez glanced
his way, her confident stride stuttered a little before she
continued on toward her destination.

John watched her as she unloaded the plates, chatted
with her customers. Allie looked from John to Inez,
and had to smile, wondering what might be brewing
between the two of them.

"John!" Allie called out, knowing he'd never notice
her as long as Inez was in the room. She waved. "Over
here."

He snapped out of his trance, walked over to join
her at the table. "Sorry I'm late. I got a last-minute
call."

"I haven't been here long." She handed him a
menu. "I appreciate you taking the time to have lunch
with me."

Giving the menu a cursory glance, he set it aside.

His gaze kept straying to Inez as if he couldn't quite help himself. Even as his obvious infatuation cheered Allie, her heart ached over the mess that was her relationship with Lucas.

"Do you and Inez know each other well?" Allie asked.

"What?" He snapped his head back toward Allie as Inez disappeared into the kitchen. "No. Just through Lucas. Actually, I hadn't seen her for years until the rehearsal dinner."

Allie reached for her water glass, took a sip, then set it down, the condensation chilling her hand. "I hope you don't mind talking to me a bit about Lucas."

John fixed his dark-brown gaze on her. "If sharing my insights about him can help things between you two, I'm sure Lucas wouldn't mind."

Allie suspected Lucas would mind very much, but she was desperate to get some insight into the moody, tortured man she'd married. "First tell me about the Calderas. How does he know them?"

John's eyes widened in surprise. "He hasn't even told you that much?" Shaking his head, he picked up his knife and tapped it against his other hand. "Lucas spent a large part of his childhood in foster care. He lived with the Calderas for several years until he turned eighteen."

The revelation didn't shock Allie, but the fact that Lucas had kept it from her did. "Why wouldn't he tell me? It was obvious Mrs. Caldera meant a great deal to him. Why wouldn't he introduce her as his foster mother?"

John sighed, setting aside the knife and locking his fingers together. "I'm not sure. He's only told me bits and pieces about that part of his life."

HOW TO PLAY:

1. With a coin, carefully scratch off the 3 gold areas on your Lucky Carnival Wheel. By doing so you have qualified to receive everything revealed—2 FREE books and a surprise gift—ABSOLUTELY FREE!

2. Send back this card and you'll receive 2 brand-new Silhouette Special Edition® novels. These books have a cover price of $4.75 each in the U.S. and $5.75 each in Canada, but they are yours ABSOLUTELY FREE.

3. There's no catch! You're under no obligation to buy anything. We charge nothing—ZERO—for your first shipment. And you don't have to make any minimum number of purchases—not even one!

4. The fact is thousands of readers enjoy receiving books by mail from the Silhouette Reader Service™. They enjoy the convenience of home delivery...they like getting the best new novels at discount prices, BEFORE they're available in stores... and they love their *Heart to Heart* subscriber newsletter featuring author news, horoscopes, recipes, book reviews and much more!

5. We hope that after receiving your free books you'll want to remain a subscriber. But the choice is yours—to continue or cancel, any time at all! So why not take us up on our invitation, with no risk of any kind. You'll be glad you did!

A surprise gift

FREE

We can't tell you what it is...but we're sure you'll like it! A

FREE GIFT!

just for playing LUCKY CARNIVAL WHEEL!

Visit us online at
www.eHarlequin.com

LUCKY Carnival Wheel

Find Out Instantly The Gifts You Get Absolutely FREE!

Scratch-off Game

Scratch off **ALL 3** Gold areas

YES! I have scratched off the 3 Gold Areas above. Please send me the 2 FREE books and gift for which I qualify! I understand I am under no obligation to purchase any books, as explained on the back and on the opposite page.

335 SDL DNXC   235 SDL DNW5

FIRST NAME	LAST NAME

ADDRESS

APT.#	CITY

STATE/PROV.	ZIP/POSTAL CODE

The Silhouette Reader Service™ — here's how it works:

Accepting your 2 free books and gift places you under no obligation to buy anything. You may keep the books and gift and return the shipping statement marked "cancel." If you do not cancel, about a month later we'll send you 6 additional novels and bill you just $3.99 each in the U.S., or $4.74 each in Canada, plus 25¢ shipping & handling per book and applicable taxes if any.* That's the complete price and — compared to cover prices of $4.75 each in the U.S. and $5.75 each in Canada—it's quite a bargain! You may cancel at any time, but if you choose to continue, every month we'll send you 6 more books, which you may either purchase at the discount price or return to us and cancel your subscription.

*Terms and prices subject to change without notice. Sales tax applicable in N.Y. Canadian residents will be charged applicable provincial taxes and GST.

BUSINESS REPLY MAIL
FIRST-CLASS MAIL   PERMIT NO. 717-003   BUFFALO, NY

POSTAGE WILL BE PAID BY ADDRESSEE

SILHOUETTE READER SERVICE
3010 WALDEN AVE
PO BOX 1867
BUFFALO NY 14240-9952

NO POSTAGE
NECESSARY
IF MAILED
IN THE
UNITED STATES

If offer card is missing write to: Silhouette Reader Service, 3010 Walden Ave., P.O. Box 1867, Buffalo, NY 14240-1867

"What has he told you?"

John shrugged. "He never knew his father. His mother drank so he went to foster homes when she couldn't take care of him. His mother died when he was young—nine or ten."

Each detail John added knotted Allie's stomach tighter. "How did she die?"

"I've never asked."

Allie doubted Lucas would answer. "And what about the scar?"

John looked uncomfortable for a moment. "An accident. That's all he would tell me."

Wrapping both hands around her water glass, Allie gripped it like a lifeline. "Why hasn't he told me any of this, John?"

John's gaze dropped to his linked hands. "What I know about Lucas I've drawn out of him over a period of years. Anytime I've probed too deep, he's told me the past has nothing to do with who he is now, so he sees no point in discussing it."

"But it has everything to do with who he is now," Allie protested. Frustration boiled inside her. "Why does he lock himself away from his friends, the people who care about him?"

"Honestly?" John took a long drink of water. "Control. As a child, he could control nothing. Everything in his life was decided by others. Now, as an adult *he* controls everything, from TaylorMade on down to his own emotions. If he loses control…"

Whatever else John might have said faded away as Inez approached with her order pad in hand. Diminutive but voluptuous, Inez managed to give Allie a warm welcoming smile and John a haughty scowl in nearly the same breath.

She pointedly focused her attention on Allie. "Can I bring you the special today? We served it to your *guapo* husband week before last when he came in for lunch."

Allie felt as if she'd had the breath knocked out of her. Lucas had been in town? He'd come and gone without seeing her? She looked up at John, saw the sympathy in his dark-brown eyes. "Did you know…" she asked him.

He studied his well-manicured hands. "He called me."

Swallowing past the hurt, Allie forced a smile for Inez. "The special sounds good to me."

Inez turned to John, cocking her hip. "What about you, *guero? La especialidad de la casa?*"

The heat steaming between the two could have started the water simmering in their glasses. When the silence stretched out, Allie cleared her throat loudly to capture their attention.

"The special's fine," John said, nearly toppling the water glasses when he slid the menus across the table. "Not too hot, please."

Her equanimity recovered, Inez smirked at John. "Wouldn't want to burn that *guero* tongue."

As Inez walked away, John ran his hand over his neat blond hair, clearly agitated. Allie smiled, grateful for the chance to focus on something other than her own problems.

"So what's going on between you two?"

John's eyes went wide. "Nothing. Me and Inez?" He barked a laugh. "Nothing."

"But you'd like there to be," Allie guessed.

John shook his head. "We're about as ill-suited as two people could be. I'm a lawyer, she hates lawyers.

She likes Latino men, I'm not Latino. Even worse, I'm *rubio*—blond.'' Even as he spoke, John's eyes strayed to Inez as she delivered an order to a table across the room.

''Have you asked her out?''

''What?'' John turned back to Allie, registered her question. ''Hell, no. She spent the entire night of the rehearsal dinner telling me every lawyer joke she knows. I wouldn't be so much of a masochist as to ask her out.''

Allie dropped the subject, returning her thoughts to her husband. During their brief engagement, in the short time they'd been married, she'd always felt one step behind Lucas, with her heart always on the defensive.

She considered what John had said—how crucial it was for Lucas to maintain control. Her own father had been much the same, although French Dickenson saw the iron fist as a man's birthright. Raised by a tyrannical father himself, French felt a man's place in society required he control the women in his family—his wife, his daughters. Thank God he hadn't passed that arrogance on to Stephen, or Anne might never have married him.

Without even meaning to, she'd fallen into the same pattern with Lucas she'd always followed with her father. Out of a desire to keep everything on an even keel, to avoid the outbursts she dreaded, she'd accepted Lucas's actions without questioning them.

She'd let him close himself off to her after they made love. She'd let him abandon her these three weeks, let him escape the pain that closeness with her seemed to expose. She'd allowed him to run her life, run her emotions just as her father had all those years.

Her father had done it by being a tyrant. Lucas accomplished the same thing by cutting himself off from her. Damned if she would let him continue. Theirs might not be a true marriage, but she at least deserved a husband that stayed home with her, spent time with her, paid her a little attention. That certainly wasn't too much to ask.

So what now? Call him? Not this afternoon at the factory; she'd have to wait until this evening when he returned to his hotel. Could she demand he come home? Cut his trip short? What reason could she give him?

I need you, Lucas.

Because she did. She needed the time spent with him, needed those hours at night talking about their day, or just sharing the companionable silence. Until now, she hadn't realized just how much she'd enjoyed those two short weeks of their marriage before they'd made love. She wanted that easy camaraderie back.

She only needed the courage to pick up the phone. As she tried to frame in her mind what she would say to Lucas, anxiety set her stomach churning. The faint nausea persisted when her food arrived. Staring down at the plate heaped with *carne asada,* rice and beans, Allie wondered how she would ever take a bite.

John was observant enough to recognize her distress. "Feeling okay?"

"I'm fine." Her hand trembling a bit, she took a sip of water, then picked up her fork. Her stomach gave another little lurch as she breathed in the aroma of *carne asada.* But with the first bite, her queasiness vanished. "Just hungry, I guess."

John caught her smile, grinned in return. "You seem in better spirits."

Reaching across the table, she touched John's hand lightly. "Thank you for everything. You've been a big help."

Suddenly ravenous, she cut another mouthful of *carne asada,* savored the deliciously seasoned beef. She pondered the coming confrontation with Lucas. At worst, her demands could drive him further away. But the man couldn't travel forever. He'd have to face her sooner or later.

She intended to make sure it was sooner. If twenty-six years as French Dickenson's daughter had taught her anything, it was grit and determination. She'd learned how to handle her father. It was time she did the same with Lucas.

Chapter Nine

Dead tired, Lucas swung the hotel door shut behind him and dropped his briefcase on the desk. His overcoat he dropped on the desk chair, not caring that it dragged on the floor. Slipping off his shoes and kicking them into the closet, he waffled over whether to shower now or wait until morning.

Morning would be soon enough. Shedding his jacket, he hung it up in the closet, then stuffed his shirt into the hotel laundry bag. Stripping down to his shorts, he staggered to the bed.

When his bleary gaze snagged on the blinking red message light, he considered leaving whatever crisis it represented until morning. But on the slim chance it might be Allie, he picked up the receiver and punched out the numbers for the message service.

When he first heard her recorded words on the voice mail, his heart slammed into overdrive. She'd called him. After days when her only contact with him had been regarding work issues, she'd actually initiated a call to him.

A beep sounded at the end of the message and Lucas realized he hadn't registered a word she'd said. For all he knew, she'd only called to inform him of some last-minute detail related to the information he'd last requested of her. His hands shook as he pressed the buttons to replay the message. Even if there was nothing personal in her call, he wanted to hear it again.

"Lucas," she said, then hesitated. "Lucas, please call me at home. No matter how late. We need to talk."

As he let the receiver slip back into its cradle, conflicting emotions battled within him—joy that she wanted to talk to him, trepidation over why. What if she'd tired of their sham of a marriage? What if she wanted her freedom?

And could he blame her? He'd treated her so shoddily the morning they'd made love, so cruelly. He'd thought only of himself, taking his pleasure in her body and then abandoning her because she'd gotten too close. The sweetness of her touch had nearly exploded the barriers between them and it had terrified him.

But that fear was nothing compared to the terror of losing Allie. He tried to shake loose the sense of dread, to tell himself Allie wouldn't leave him. He had only to dial his home number and speak to her to allay his fears. But his hands seemed reluctant to move. Even as he assured himself Allie wasn't calling it quits, he couldn't shake the sense of impending doom. But what could be worse than Allie leaving?

Something deep inside him knew the answer. A little voice he'd struggled for years to keep walled in. A part of him that had grown stronger during this brief time with Allie.

Too much pain lay in that direction if he gave that voice credence. Much easier to keep it buried.

Cursing his own cowardice, Lucas lifted the receiver again and punched out his phone number. It rang only once before Allie answered with a breathless, "Hello?"

"It's me," he said, keeping his tone brusque. "What did you need?"

She dragged in a deep breath. "You, Lucas. I need you."

He had to squeeze his eyes shut against the thrill of joy that burst within him. It took a moment to find the words, to keep them even and neutral. "What do you mean?"

If his intentionally obtuse question irritated her, she didn't let it show. "I need you here. I need you home."

A sudden irrational terror shot up his spine. "Are you sick? Are you hurt?"

She laughed, a soft sound. "No, Lucas. I just…" The silence stretched. "I miss you."

His defenses seemed to crumble in that moment, like a wall with its keystone removed. He gathered his control more tightly around him. "I still have business here."

He didn't; it was ridiculous of him to say so. In fact, the New Jersey VPs had grown increasingly testy at his micro-managing. Accustomed to much more latitude from him, having their every move evaluated had frayed tempers today.

"Please," she said, a wealth of sweet entreaty in her voice. "Please come home."

Home. Come home. He felt his walls quake again as

that comforting word echoed inside him. Until that moment, he'd never quite thought of the palatial estate he occupied as a home. It had always simply been a symbol of his wealth, his power in the world.

But now it was a home. Because of her. Because of Allie.

With the blossoming emotions inside him, his foundation seemed to shift, to grow unstable even as a stronger base revealed itself. Not wanting to consider the implications, he tamped those unwelcome feelings back down.

"I can probably wrap things up here tomorrow, take the red-eye back."

She released a pent-up breath, the sound teasing his ear. "Shall I make the reservations for you?"

"I'll have someone here take care of it. I won't know for certain the time until tomorrow. I might even have to delay another day."

"Oh." Her disappointment bit into him. "I'll see you when you get home, then."

"Yes. See you then."

The silent moments ticked by and he wondered if she'd hung up. Then she said, "Lucas?"

The tones of his name spoken by her curled around him like a caress. He shut his eyes to savor the sound. "Yes?"

"Thank you. Thank you for coming home."

She said goodbye then and he waited until he heard the phone disconnect. Then he lowered the receiver, letting it slip from his hand. Images of Allie crowded in, soft and warm in bed, the melody of her voice trembling on the phone line.

God, he wanted her. He ached for her, physi
mentally, emotionally. Everything about tha

her screamed danger, yet he couldn't turn back the desire that ripped through him.

Hope had long ago died, had decayed and gone to dust. But somehow Allie urged it to life, bucking the impossibility of renewal. Each stone he set back into place in that wall around the most tender part of his soul she took away with nothing more than a sigh, a smile.

Without thought, Lucas reached for the phone again. Digging in the nightstand for the directory, he flipped to the Yellow Pages for the airline listings. In five more minutes, he'd scheduled himself on the first morning flight home.

Home. He was going home. To Allie.

Sinking onto the bed, he knew he wouldn't sleep. Instead he lay there, impatient and content all at once as he let his thoughts drift, again and again, to his wife.

The next two weeks passed in a haze of giddy excitement for Allie. As if to make up for his time away, Lucas made every effort to be with her as much as possible. He had her block out the lunch hour, asking her to keep her schedule clear for both of them during that time. They would spend that hour uninterrupted at a local restaurant, or they'd brown-bag it and eat outside at the picnic tables set up for TaylorMade employees. The unusually warm early-November weather only added to the pleasure of time spent with him.

He ___ her often, a hand at the small of her back ___ her through a door, his fingers wrapped ___ n they walked side by side after lunch. ___ sion still persisted between them, ___ inside Allie. She could see it in his ___ way his hand would linger on her arm as he helped her into the car. There were moments she thought his passion would leap out of control, thought the tempest in him would explode. She ached for the explosion, but the tight leash he kept on his desires never loosened.

Even without intimacy, the marriage finally seemed real to Allie. Much as her body wanted otherwise, she could live without the physical aspect to their union as long as she had Lucas at her side.

Now, sitting at her desk, counting down the minutes until lunchtime, she couldn't keep a smile from curving her lips. Lucas was spending the morning in Modesto again, but they'd arranged to meet at *Cocina Caldera* in another hour. He'd e-mailed her twice to confirm, and now she couldn't seem to think of anything else.

When the elevator door opened, Allie's heart leapt with hope that Lucas had returned unexpectedly early. But it was only Randy Sato, one of the engineers from Research and Development.

"Allie," he called out as he approached her desk, "can you look up the date of the SoftDunk planning meeting last month? I misplaced my notes."

She brought up the calendar on her laptop, flipped back through the weeks searching for the meeting date. "Looks like October nineteenth," she told Randy.

He flashed her a grin of thanks, then headed for the coffee room. Allie glanced at the time on her laptop display, sighing over the endless minutes that still stretched until she could leave for lunch. About to close the calendar, her gaze strayed to earlier in the week in mid-October.

She registered two things in quick succession—the mid-October date she and Lucas had made love and the asterisk entered on the calendar six days prior. As she stared at it, the asterisk seemed to glow and brighten on the screen.

A habit from her midteens when her cycles were terribly irregular, ranging from nearly nonexistent to embarrassingly long and heavy, she still used an asterisk to mark the start of her period. With so many visits to the gynecologist back then, she'd needed a reliable way to recall the date.

Once she'd entered her twenties, her cycles had inexplicably kicked into unswerving regularity. She started on nearly the same date each month.

Except this month. Full of trepidation, Allie checked today's date, did a quick calculation. Her stomach, never very dependable these days, did a queasy flip-flop. Good God, she was over a week late.

It couldn't be. She and Lucas had made love immediately after she'd finished her period. She couldn't have been fertile then.

She couldn't possibly be pregnant.

Struggling to contain her rising alarm, she tried to remember her sister Sherril's complaints about the first trimester of pregnancy. The nausea she had in spades. But her breasts felt only slightly tender—that could signal her imminent period. Her moodiness could be explained, as well—the last several weeks had been rough emotionally.

Looking around her, praying her suspicions didn't show on her face, she discovered Helen watching her with bemusement one desk over. When Allie's gaze met hers, the older woman smiled. "Still pretty overwhelming, I suppose."

She knows! Oh, my God, she knows! Allie scrambled for a response. "I…I don't…"

Helen continued to beam. "He can't be an easy man

to be married to, but it's obvious how much you two love each other.''

Too caught up in relief that Helen hadn't somehow read her mind, it took Allie a moment to absorb what the older woman had said. Helen thought Lucas loved his wife, that she loved Lucas? Allie nearly denied it, then reminded herself that was exactly the impression she and Lucas should give.

She managed a smile. "Yes, we're very happy."

A call diverted Helen's attention, leaving Allie to stew over her current predicament. Could she be? Could she actually be…? And if she was…

What would Lucas say? What would he do? A child was the one thing he professed to want more than anything. If she were nurturing that precious gift inside her, would he lower the barriers between them, let her break through the impenetrable shell he hid behind?

Even as joy struggled to take form inside her, cold reality crept in and gave her its answer. Lucas could control an adoption, manage it like a business decision. But a child of his own flesh, growing inside her—it would be as if his control had been snatched away. How would he cope with that? Would he respond with anger? Or would he simply retreat further into himself?

Tears pricked at her eyes as exultation warred with heartache. To pray that she was mistaken, that she and Lucas had not made a child, hurt more than she could imagine. But to bring a baby into their false marriage would be terribly wrong.

Another realization exploded within her. She and Lucas had agreed to a temporary union. If she was carrying his child, how could she possibly leave it behind? She couldn't, not when it was part of her flesh and blood. Not when the man who had fathered the child had come to mean more to her than even her next breath.

As the truth settled in on her, a fist seemed to clutch at her heart. She dropped her head in her hands, closing out the buzz of the office around her. She tried to grasp what her heart had finally managed to communicate to her.

She loved Lucas. Without meaning to, without trying to, she'd fallen in love with her moody, arrogant husband. She'd followed precisely in her mother's footsteps, something she'd sworn never to do. How could she have let herself stumble down that same path?

Allie raised her head, locked her hands together on her desk. Images drifted in her mind's eye like a mental collage. Lucas smiling across the table from her at dinner, an unguarded tenderness in his eyes. Lucas pouring her coffee in the morning, taking care to measure out exactly the amount of cream and sugar she preferred. Lucas lost in a nightmare, reaching out to her, finding comfort in her touch.

She loved him not in spite of his arrogance, but because of it—because she knew he used it to mask the pain of his past. And in spite of himself, in spite of the walls he hid behind, there was a part of Lucas reaching out to her. It was that part she had learned to love.

But she couldn't possibly tell him. If news of her pregnancy would send Lucas running for cover, her admission of her love for him would certainly finish the job.

She wouldn't tell him. Not about loving him. And until she knew for certain, she'd keep silent about the possibility of a baby, too. She'd pick up a home pregnancy test this evening on her way home from the office, hide it in her room. Just as well she and Lucas had driven in in separate cars today.

She checked the clock again, saw it was time to head for the restaurant. Her hands shook as she powered off her computer and gathered her purse and sweater. She gave Helen a wan smile as she headed for the elevator, felt intense relief when she saw the car was empty. Sinking against the wall as the doors slid shut, she prayed for the strength to get through the next few days.

As she drove the Volvo across town to *Cocina Caldera,* resolve built inside her. If she did carry Lucas's child, she would fight for their marriage to continue. She wanted her child in a home with two parents. Even if he never learned to love her, somehow she would teach Lucas to love their son or daughter.

That would simply have to be enough.

Seated across the table from her in *Cocina Caldera,* Lucas thought he had never seen such turbulent emotions in Allie. One moment she looked troubled, as if the weight of the world were on her shoulders. The next, she couldn't seem to stop smiling, and the curve of her lips, the giddy joy lighting her eyes set off an answering happiness in his own heart. He'd stayed away from her for nearly a month, he'd deprived himself of such sweetness—he'd been such a jackass.

And the hurt he must have caused her—he hated to think of it. That she could so easily forgive him was a gift he didn't deserve. He had to find a way to make it up to her, but even the most lavish treasures would be inadequate.

She frowned and looked away and he couldn't help

himself; he reached across the table to take her hand. "What is it?"

A startled expression flashed across her face. "I…oh…" she stammered. "Nothing. I mean…" She looked away briefly, then back at him. "Are you sure about Thanksgiving? Going to my sister's, I mean."

The non sequitur threw him for a loop, for a moment distracted him from the fact that she was hiding something. He considered pushing the issue, but why grill her about why she looked so happy? He should simply be grateful that she was.

Stroking his thumb across the back of her hand, he assured her, "Thanksgiving with your family will be fine."

Her fingers fluttered against his palm, elevating his heart rate. "Because if there's something you usually do for the holiday—"

"What I usually do," he said, tightening his hand around hers, "is catch up on work. I can get quite a bit done around the office when no one else is there."

The sympathy in her soft green eyes curled inside him, at once an ache and a balm. "You don't have any family at all to spend the day with?"

He shrugged, as if it meant nothing to him. "I've shared dinner with John's family in the Bay area one or two years."

"What about the Calderas? You must have spent Thanksgiving with them a few times."

"The Calderas?" he asked carefully.

Color rose in her cheeks. "I had lunch with John while you were gone. We talked."

So used to protecting his past, he felt immediately on the defensive. "What did he tell you?"

She tipped her chin up. "That you spent a great deal

of time in foster homes, one of which was the Calderas.''

He should be outraged, incensed she had pried into his past. But faced with Allie's earnest gaze, her gentle smile, it seemed ridiculous to deny the importance of his relationship with Teresa and Inez. He felt another shifting inside him, another chink opening in his armor. But instead of filling the space back up, it seemed so much easier to let a little bit of Allie in.

He closed her hand in both of his. ''I shared Thanksgiving with the Calderas for several years, both while I lived with them and once I moved out. But when Teresa's husband Enrique passed away, their Thanksgiving day shifted to one of the cousin's houses. I have a standing invitation there, but I scarcely know that part of the family.''

''A little awkward, huh?''

Her understanding set him at ease. ''Yes. And since I never celebrated the holiday as a child, it's never been a big deal.''

Her eyes went wide. ''Never celebrated Thanksgiving?''

''Never. Not until I was thirteen. When I lived with the Calderas.''

She seemed to struggle to absorb that fact. ''But Christmas—you must have celebrated Christmas.''

All those years of hope and disappointment shouldn't matter anymore. Seeing the decorations go up at school, in even the poorest homes in his rundown neighborhood and knowing his mother would never do the same in his own home shouldn't still hurt. But opening himself to Allie seemed to rebuild a path to that old pain, seemed to tear away the protection he'd built around it.

All at once the anger returned and he wanted to lash out. How could he, knowing Allie only probed because she cared? That caring was an integral part of her nature, as natural for her as her next breath.

"I don't know what John told you, but I suspect our lives were very different, yours and mine." Swallowing his irritation, he forced himself to voice the words with cool neutrality. "No Christmases, Allie. No Thanksgivings, no birthdays."

"Oh, Lucas—"

"Please, don't," he bit out, jaw aching with tension. "It doesn't matter. Not anymore."

It was a lie, a bald-faced lie. Allie could see it in his face. She had to tread carefully. "But the Calderas must have—"

"They tried." He glanced away, his tone cool. "But by then those days had no meaning to me."

Anger flooded Allie that the world had been so cruel, had torn apart a young boy's hopes, leaving none for the man he'd become. She felt angry, too, at Lucas's mother, a faceless woman who had no doubt fought her own demons.

An idea burst into Allie's mind, a way to give back to Lucas something he'd lost all those years. Before she could second-guess herself, Allie leapt ahead.

"What if TaylorMade hosted a Christmas party for under-privileged kids?" she blurted out.

Lucas's brow furrowed. "A Christmas party?"

She nodded, thinking quickly. "We could hold it in the company cafeteria. Have employees volunteer to decorate and to entertain the children."

"During company time?"

"It wouldn't have to be. Maybe the Friday before Christmas, right after close of business."

He stared at her steadily, his expression doubtful. "What about gifts? Christmas presents for the kids— would TaylorMade provide those, as well?"

Was he looking for an excuse to say no? Allie's stomach fluttered and she had a sudden keen sense of the life within her. In that moment she knew she didn't need a pregnancy test to know the truth.

Her impulsive suggestion of a Christmas party suddenly took on a tremendous significance. Somehow the celebration, the baby inside her, her hopeless love for Lucas had all become tangled together. She would make sure the holiday party happened if she had to organize every last detail herself.

Determination goaded her. "TaylorMade wouldn't have to buy the gifts. Let the employees. We'll put up a 'wishing tree' in the lobby. Hang requests on it from local needy kids and let the employees pick the presents they want to buy."

"What if one of the children gets missed?"

His quiet words were nearly her undoing. Tears sprang to her eyes as she thought of Lucas as a boy, wishing for presents that never came.

"They won't. I promise." She rubbed away the wetness in her eyes. "If any kids don't get picked, I'll buy their gifts."

"No."

"No?" He wouldn't let her throw the party?

"TaylorMade will purchase the extra gifts."

Joy burst inside her. "I can give a Christmas party?"

"Of course. Just work up a budget, give it to me next week."

She laughed at his businesslike tone. "What's my budget?"

"I'll leave it to you to decide." He looked away a moment, his gaze unfocused as if he were a million miles away from the busy, bustling restaurant. Then he returned his attention to her. "I'd like you to talk to Teresa. She's not a foster parent anymore, but she knows who still is. I'd like to invite local foster children to the party."

He seemed embarrassed, unsure of her reaction. Allie knew what it had taken for him to make the request, to expose that bit of his past. She tried to think of a way to assure him, to make him understand how much his generosity moved her.

In the end, she just smiled, lifted his hand to her lips. She pressed a kiss to the back of his hand, wishing all that lay in her heart could be transmitted to him through the contact.

I love you, she said silently, with her eyes, with her very soul. *I love you, Lucas Taylor.*

Chapter Ten

With the arrival of Allie's cousins from Southern California, the annual Dickenson Thanksgiving gathering reached its usual peak of noise and chaos. The cacophony never failed to fill Allie with joy and this year she had even more reason for happiness.

She was pregnant with Lucas's child. She had verified it with two home pregnancy tests taken on two separate mornings. And despite the uncertainty of her future with the father of her child, her spirits soared at the prospect of the new life she carried within her.

Confirmation of her pregnancy had lent her strength. She would find a way through this, would find the right words to say to Lucas. Somehow, it would all come out right.

Now she sat on the living-room sofa with her newest niece, Brianna, snuggled in her arms. The five-week-old infant was a precious slight weight as she slept on, oblivious to the din. Allie imagined her own child swaddled like Brianna, gazing up at her with Lucas's serious gray eyes. She pictured herself bringing the baby to her breast, Lucas looking on with pride.

She glanced over at her husband anxiously. He'd seemed increasingly overwhelmed as the crowd in Sherril and Pete's house swelled in number. For the past hour, he'd been standing in the corner of the living room, leaning against the bookcase as he watched the commotion around him. To anyone else he would seem aloof, but Allie knew differently. Lucas wanted to be part of the constant motion in the room. He just didn't know how.

His gaze sought her out and she smiled at him, putting her whole heart into the gesture. He relaxed fractionally, a wisp of an answering smile curving his mouth.

Daniel, Sherril's five-year-old, seemed as lost as Lucas as he sat Indian-style on the floor near the blaring television. Elbows on knees, chin planted in his hands—Allie had never seen a longer face.

She met Lucas's gaze again, then glanced significantly down at Daniel. When she returned her focus to Lucas, he seemed startled at first when he absorbed her message. He looked down at Daniel then back at Allie as if to ask, *What do I do?* She smiled and shrugged, leaving it to him.

Allie thought he might just ignore the boy, but Lucas surprised her. Stepping carefully over six-month-old Juliana, Lucas hunkered down next to Daniel. Allie could see Lucas's lips moving as he talked to the five-year-old, but couldn't hear what he said over the steady noise.

Daniel's face brightened and he said something in

response to Lucas. Lucas seemed to hesitate before he nodded. He straightened as Daniel scrambled to his feet. When Daniel captured Lucas's hand, Allie could see her husband's awkwardness from across the room. But he recovered quickly, closing his hand around the little boy's as they made their way back to the bookcase.

As Lucas lowered himself to the floor, Daniel quickly scanned the bottom two shelves of books. He pulled out two in quick succession, considered, then grabbed a third. In another moment, he'd settled in next to Lucas, the books straddling their laps.

Allie's heart seemed to expand in her chest as she watched Lucas and Daniel take turns reading the books. Lucas listened to Daniel with his trademark single-minded focus, helping with a difficult word, pointing out something interesting on the page. Daniel's shoulders grew straighter as he read beside his new uncle, his pride in his reading skills evident.

Then Daniel tipped his head up to Lucas and asked him a question. While the little boy waited, his expression expectant, Lucas seemed stunned. Only for an instant, then he nodded and spread out his arms in a welcoming gesture. Daniel climbed into Lucas's lap, snuggling against his broad chest. With his arms around the boy, Lucas leaned against the bookcase as they continued to read.

Tears brimmed in Allie's eyes as she watched. Lucas's initial awkwardness had vanished. His contentment shone in the relaxed line of his body, the ease in his shoulders as he helped Daniel turn the pages.

Sherril sat next to Allie, folding her legs under her. "That man will make a wonderful father."

Warmth spread inside Allie as she considered the

treasure growing inside her. "I think you're right. Until just now, I don't think I'd ever seen him interact with children."

Sherril sighed as she watched Daniel bask in the glow of his uncle's undivided attention. "It's been hard for Danny these last few weeks. He got to be the baby for so long." She tapped Brianna lightly on her tiny nose. "Then this monster came to take his place."

As if sensing her mother's presence, Brianna shifted in Allie's arms and woke. The baby gave Allie a worried look, then let loose an indignant yowl.

With gentle hands, Sherril lifted her youngest from Allie's arms. "She goes from slumber to cranky in one point two seconds. I'd better go change her and feed her."

Allie pitched her voice higher to be heard over Brianna's hearty screams. "What can I do to help with dinner?"

Rising, Sherril propped Brianna over her shoulder. "Check on Pete. Make sure he hasn't massacred the bird."

As Sherril worked her way through the obstacle course of children and adults draped on the floor or sitting in chairs, Allie headed for the kitchen. She looked over her shoulder to see Lucas watching her leave. He bent down to say something in Daniel's ear, then the two of them got to their feet.

In the kitchen, the noise level dropped considerably. Clinging to Lucas's hand, Daniel seemed in seventh heaven. "We're gonna help, Aunt Allie," he announced. "Uncle Lucas said."

"Go check with your father, Daniel," Lucas told him. "Ask him what to do."

Daniel skipped across the kitchen to where Pete

wrestled with a massive turkey. Lucas turned to face Allie, a strange mixture of emotions playing across his face. His hands opened and closed in a restless pattern.

She stepped in close to him, threaded her arms around his waist. The muscles of his back felt rock-hard under his turtleneck. With only the barest hesitation, he wrapped his arms around her, bringing her into a tight embrace. He took a long breath, then as he released it, tension seeped from his body.

"My family can be a bit much," she murmured into his ear.

"An understatement." His soft chuckle sifted through her hair. "But no fighting. No arguments."

She laughed. "You haven't seen us play Scrabble yet. Pete has a nasty habit of throwing in words only another surgeon would know."

His hands skimmed her back, warming her through her thick wool sweater. She imagined them holding each other like this when she was further along in her pregnancy. Would he press his palm against her belly, feel for a kick, send his love to his baby with the contact?

Or would their child growing inside her give him another excuse to keep his distance from her? She wished she could predict his reaction, could see the future and know how their lives would turn out.

"Hey, you two," Pete called out, brandishing a drumstick. "You here to neck in the kitchen or are you going to give us a hand?"

Lucas pulled away from her, leaving her feeling slightly bereft. For a man used to calling the shots in his own corporation, he took Pete's orders in good humor, locating the platters for the turkey, lifting the heavy pot of boiled potatoes from the stove. Allie su-

pervised Daniel in composing the relish tray and filling
the bread basket.

By the time they all seated themselves around the
dining-room table, rubbing elbows in the tight space,
Allie would have sworn Lucas had been a member of
the family for years. He joked with Pete about his carv-
ing job, teased Daniel about the towering mountain of
food the boy had piled on his plate, complimented
Sherril on how quickly she'd recovered her figure. His
openness both astonished and pleased Allie and hope
bubbled up inside her.

Still, from time to time, she caught glimpses of the
little boy in Lucas's face as he gazed around the table.
It was almost as if he couldn't quite believe he was
part of this noisy, happy group, as if at any moment it
would be snatched away. At those times, she would
reach for his hand under the table, give him a reassur-
ing squeeze.

When they'd all eaten their fill and the children had
abandoned the adults for a video in the living room, a
rare quiet descended around the table. Sherril leaned
against her husband, Brianna in the crook of her arm.
Not sure of her reception, Allie rested her head tentatively against Lucas's shoulder. To her delight, he
curved his arm around her, nestling her against him.

Stephen, his hand linked with his wife's, smiled at
Allie. "So what's this big surprise you've been teasing
us with all week?"

"I almost forgot." Although loathe to leave Lucas's
side, she eased herself away. "I'll go get it."

Hurrying into Sherril's and Pete's bedroom where
she'd left her purse, she retrieved what she'd mentally
referred to as her "Thanksgiving project." A slim,
comb-bound book full of family photographs of

Thanksgivings past, she'd assembled it in secret at the office.

"I hope you don't mind, Lucas," she said as she re-entered the dining room. "I used TaylorMade's scanner and color printer. Jim in the print shop helped me put it together."

She handed the book to Sherril first. "It's a Thanksgiving memory book," she told her sister. "Everyone's in there—the ones that are here, the ones that are gone."

Sherril's eyes grew misty as she flipped through the book of family photos, stopping at the page that featured their mother and father. Once Sherril finished with the book, it was passed from hand to hand around the table.

Finally it was Lucas's turn. He laid the book before him on the table, turned the pages. Allie had included captions under each photo, some humorous, some touching. She explained the relationships to Lucas and he listened with polite attention.

When he reached the wedding portrait Stephen had taken at the church, he gazed at it for a long time. "You were so beautiful that day," he murmured. He turned to her, his gaze soft. "Almost as beautiful as you are now."

He leaned over to brush a kiss on her cheek, ignoring Pete's catcall. Then he turned to the last page of the book.

The moment he saw the picture, she saw hot color rise in his face. Allie realized she'd miscalculated badly. "Lucas..."

He turned to her, his rage burning in his metal-gray eyes. "Where did you get this picture?"

The tendons stood out in his hands; she tried to

soothe them away with her touch. "From Teresa. I asked if she had a picture of your mother and she—"

"You had no right! No damn right!"

He ripped out the page, crumpling it as he tossed the book across the table. Shoving the balled paper in his pocket, he sprang to his feet, nearly toppling his chair. In three angry strides, he'd left the dining room. She heard Daniel call out "Uncle Lucas!" then the slam of the front door.

Her eyes filling with tears, she threw a quick apologetic glance at her sister and brother, then ran after her husband. As soon as she stepped outside, the damp November air cut straight to the bone. She looked up and down the street, searching for him.

He hadn't gone far. His head down, shoulders hunched, he leaned against a lamppost three houses down. The lamp's mist-haloed light cast him in shadow, starkly illuminated the rigid line of his body.

Allie approached cautiously, shivering in the cold. When she reached his side, she curved her hand around his arm, a featherlight touch. He whirled to face her, stared at her as if she were a stranger.

"Lucas...?"

He grasped her arms, pulling her to him, holding her tightly as he tipped back her head. Almost before she could take a breath, he lowered his mouth to hers. His rough kiss, the explicit thrusting of his tongue snatched the air from her lungs, sent heat searing through her veins.

There was a moment of fear when she thought his anger would take him too far. Then his kiss gentled, still on the outer edges of civilized, but less desperate. He pressed her back against the lamppost, his hips grinding into hers, the hard length of his arousal burning against her.

She pulled back, gasped for breath. "Lucas, we can't." She gulped in the cold moist air. "Not here."

His chest heaved, a mix of passion and anger in his eyes. "Get your things. We're going home."

"But Lucas—"

"Now," he ordered.

Beginning to feel angry herself, she opened her mouth, ready to argue with him. One look at his set jaw and stony expression and Allie knew she'd get nowhere with him. She hurried inside the house, pausing in the dining room where her family still sat, no doubt stunned by Lucas's outburst.

"I'm sorry," she said, her gaze skimming quickly around the table. "We have to go."

She hurried on into Sherril and Pete's bedroom for her purse and their jackets. Sherril called her name and followed, watched from the door as Allie dug through the pile of coats and jackets on the bed.

"What is wrong with him?" Sherril asked.

Feeling the onset of tears, Allie turned her back to her sister as she continued her search. "Nothing. He's just not feeling well."

If she thought she could hide her tears from her sister, she was mistaken. Moving into the room, Sherril grabbed her, turned her toward her. "Damn, he's got you crying. What did he do to you?" Her voice dropped to a harsh whisper. "Is he hurting you?"

Of course he was, but not in the way Sherril meant. "No," she told her sister emphatically. "Lucas just…" How could she possibly explain her husband to Sherril when she didn't understand him herself? Finally spotting their jackets, she untangled them from the pile, gave her sister a peck on the cheek and hurried back outside.

Lucas waited for her on the porch, his warm breath roiling in the cold air. Slinging his jacket over the porch rail, he held hers for her while she slipped it on, then donned his own.

He cupped her elbow, led her to the Mercedes. Once they were inside and had pulled away from Sherril and Pete's house, Allie tried again. "Lucas—"

Braking at a stoplight, he turned to her, his hard gaze quelling her words. In spite of herself, Allie felt intimidated by his harshness. It was too reminiscent of episodes with her father, and she hated the feeling.

She tipped up her chin in open defiance. "When we get home, then." She kept her eyes locked with his, daring him to object.

His gaze burned into her a heartbeat longer, then he faced forward again, stepped on the accelerator when the light turned green. They didn't say another word the rest of the drive home.

He followed her into the house silently, tossed his car keys on the kitchen counter, took her jacket and hung it with his in the coat closet. Then he turned without a word toward the stairs.

Damned if she would let him escape without a confrontation. "Lucas!" she called out sharply.

He hesitated only an instant before moving on. Anger bursting inside her, Allie raced toward the stairs, took them two at a time. "Lucas, I won't let you run away!"

He reached the landing, headed for his room. One step behind him, Allie grabbed the sleeve of his turtleneck. "For God's sake, Lucas, tell me what's wrong!"

He rounded on her then, his expression so fierce Allie took an involuntary step back. "Who gave you the right?" he rasped out. "To expose my past, to invade my privacy?"

She tightened her grip on him. "Is this about your mother's picture?"

He flung out his arm in denial, dislodging her hand. "That woman had no right to be called anyone's mother. To include her with your family pictures was the worst kind of joke."

He tried to turn away again, but Allie put both hands on his arm. With all her strength, she dragged him back toward her. "Lucas, I'm sorry. I never meant to hurt you. I only wanted you to feel—"

"No." His hand flew up, covered her mouth to stop the words. "That was your mistake, Allie. I don't want to feel." His hand stroked across her mouth, cupped her cheek. "Except this."

Fingers diving into her hair, he eased her head back, covered her mouth with his. When she raised her hands to his chest to push him away, he captured them both in one of his, relentlessly moving his mouth against hers.

Then the kiss changed from an angry assault to skilled seduction. Even as his hands loosened on hers, giving her the option of freedom, the pressure of his mouth softened. Whispering along her jaw to her throat, the shell of her ear, his practiced touch drove a moan from Allie.

In one fluid movement, he hooked one arm under her knees, the other at her shoulders to lift her. Pushing open the door to his room, he carried her inside and shut the door behind them. The light of a bedside lamp illuminated the large room with a soft yellow glow.

He set her on her feet beside the bed, one hand trailing down her body as he covered her face with kisses. He brushed his lips softly against hers, from side to side, his fingers massaging, sending a chill up her spine. She shivered, unable to hold back the reaction.

His hands roamed down her body, leaving searing heat in their wake. "Undress for me," he said hoarsely.

His quicksilver gaze locked with hers, and her breath caught in her throat. She didn't have the strength to deny him. Keeping her eyes fixed on his, she slipped out of her shoes, pushed off her black wool slacks and her black-and-silver sweater. He watched her every move, his chest rising and falling in an uneven cadence.

When she reached behind her to unhook her bra, he stopped her. "Let me." One fingertip tracing along her ribcage to her back, he released the hooks, slowly drew the straps from her shoulders. He brought his hands around the front again, his knuckles grazing the tender undersides of her breasts.

His fingers dipped inside her panties, drifted along the elastic at her waist. "I have protection tonight."

Even as she trembled in response, guilt lanced through her. She had to tell him it no longer mattered. That she was already pregnant, expecting his child.

But looking into his eyes, courage failed her. After all the emotions of the evening, there was no telling what his reaction would be.

Instead she put her hands over his, pushing down. As he removed her panties, he let his knuckles skim down the skin of her thighs, her calves, her ankles. She stepped out of her panties, standing before him naked, in body and emotions.

Kneeling at her feet, his mouth swept across her belly, teasing, tasting. When she couldn't hold back a ripple of reaction, he gripped her hips tightly, keeping her still. Then his lips brushed across the nest of curls at the V of her thighs, his tongue dipping in briefly.

She threw her head back with a gasp. As pleasurable as the sensations were, she wanted him to rise so she could feel his body pressing against the length of her. But when she tugged at his hands, he resisted. He just splayed his fingers out wider, his thumbs stretching to part her folds.

Now his onslaught grew more fierce, his tongue laving wet heat over and around her sensitive nub. His lovemaking seemed almost ruthless, as if he demanded control of even her pleasure. If her mind wanted to object, to slow him down, to ask to participate in the give and take, her body would have none of that. With each stroke of Lucas's tongue, the fire inside her flared ever higher into a devastating conflagration.

As climax hit, crashing through her like storm-fed surf, she moaned a long low note and nearly collapsed. If not for his strong arms holding her up, her legs would have given way. He held her while she fell apart, his lips still pressed intimately to her, drinking up each convulsive shudder.

Finally, he rose slowly, keeping his hands on her to steady her. She swayed slightly as his gaze swept her body. "Get into bed."

Even as she complied, climbing under the covers while the last of her trembling pleasure faded, doubt assailed her. Something felt wrong here, something in the tenor of Lucas's passion, a mystery behind his arousal that teased her to decipher it.

He undressed quickly, barely taking his eyes from her as he jerked open the drawer of the nightstand be-

side the bed and pulled out a foil packet. He ripped
open the condom, applied it with shaking hands.

When he pulled back the covers, one hand fisted
around the bedding, the tendons standing out sharply
as he strafed her body with his molten silver gaze. Then
he climbed into bed, covered her body with his. His
heated skin burned her as he parted her legs with his.
He kissed her, his tongue thrusting inside her mouth as
his pelvis mimicked the sensual act.

The hard length of his arousal jutted against her
thighs, and she felt breathless anticipating their joining.
But when she moved her legs to allow him easy passage inside her, he suddenly stilled.

He dipped his head, buried his face in her throat. "I
want you, Allie," he said harshly. "I want you."

Allie stroked the length of his back, her fingers gentle over the rough scar. "I want you, too, Lucas."

He kept his face hidden. "It isn't right. I
shouldn't…"

She brought her hands up to his head, urged him up
to look at her. "Lucas, what is it?"

Finally he met her gaze. "Allie," he said, her name
a harsh whisper. "I'm sorry. For what happened at
your sister's. For the way I…"

He glanced away briefly as if searching for strength.
Then his gaze met hers again.

"It was all too much for me. The noise, the laughter,
the…love and caring." He dragged in a breath. "I
never had that. At least until the Calderas and by then
it was too late."

How could it ever be too late to be loved? "They
care for you, Lucas." Her thumbs stroked the tense line
of his jaw. "You're part of our family now."

In his face, frank disbelief warred with a young

boy's hope. Silence throbbed in the air between them, one beat, two. "Stay with me tonight, Allie," he rasped finally.

She would stay with him forever if he asked. But she knew that was more than he could offer. So she just nodded, raised up to press a gentle kiss against his lips.

He moved away from her long enough to dispose of the condom, then he gathered her in his arms. Although he was still obviously aroused, he just held her, as if she were the most precious treasure in the world.

He might not love her, but in that moment, Allie felt cherished. With his warmth seeping into her, she drifted off to sleep.

When she woke, it was barely dawn, the watery winter light sifting through the shutters. Lucas still had her body tucked in close to his, his strong arms holding her close. His breath warmed the back of her neck with each exhalation, the slow, steady rhythm telling her he still slept.

She wanted to lie like this forever, skin to skin, secure in his embrace. But the first twinges of early-morning queasiness had started up; she'd need something in her stomach soon. Besides her body's imperative, a quick glance at the bedside clock told her she'd need to get up soon to be on time meeting Sherril and Stephen this morning. They'd moved their usual Sunday visit with their father to today.

Still, she hated to leave Lucas's warmth, hated to risk waking him. She gave herself another five minutes, then her recalcitrant stomach became too insistent to be ignored. Easing Lucas's hand from her waist, she carefully extricated herself from the circle of his arms.

But not carefully enough. He stirred, reached out for her, eyes still closed. "Come back to bed."

"I have to go." Sitting on the edge of the bed, shivering in her nakedness, she took his hand. "We're visiting my father today."

"It's not Sunday," he muttered.

"We changed the day because of Thanksgiving." Goosebumps rose on her arms and it took everything in her not to climb back into bed with him.

"I'll go with you."

Pain twisted in her heart. His mind still fogged with sleep, Lucas sounded more like a vulnerable boy than the hard-edged man she knew. His first time ever to ask to accompany her, how could she tell him no? And yet she still felt the need to protect her father's dignity.

"Not this time." She lightly stroked his arm from wrist to elbow. "Another time."

He frowned, his brow furrowing. Leaning in, Allie kissed him on the temple, easing away the lines of tension. Her cheek pressed against his, she waited until his even breathing signaled her he'd fallen asleep again.

When she rose to her feet, her stomach rebelled at the quick movement. Leaving her clothes behind, she hurried to her room for her robe, then downstairs to the kitchen. A handful of crackers took the immediate edge off her queasiness, at least enough to hold her until she met her sister and brother for breakfast.

As she stood in the quiet kitchen, the gloomy overcast sending muted light through the windows, she faced the fact she couldn't hold off forever telling Lucas about her pregnancy. It could change everything— his adoption plans, their marriage agreement.

It could also destroy the little bit of progress they'd

made in growing closer, in Lucas opening up to her. Yet the longer she waited, the more angry he might be that she'd kept it a secret from him.

Damned if you do and damned if you don't. Releasing a gust of air from her lungs, she put away the packet of crackers and left the kitchen. As she climbed the stairs, she did a quick mental calculation. With any luck, she wouldn't begin to show for three or four more weeks. Waiting would give her that much more time to keep chipping away at Lucas's walls, to reach the heart he kept so well hidden. He might never love her, but if he at least learned to care for her a little, it would make it all that much easier for him to love his child.

She'd tell him by Christmas. It would be part of her holiday gift to him.

The postponement relieved her, but all that day, during breakfast and her visit with her father, she could never quite let go of a nagging sense of guilt.

Chapter Eleven

By the third week of December, Lucas barely recognized his own home. A holly wreath decorated the front door, a massive tree blocked the view from the living-room window and garlands of fir festooned the walls. Every branch down to the last twig of the ten-foot spruce glittered with ornaments. Santas, snowmen and reindeer filled every inch of space on the living-room tables, dining-room sideboard and even the dresser in Allie's bedroom.

He supposed he should feel relieved she'd left his room untouched. But somehow it seemed bare in contrast to the gaudy splendor of the rest of the house. In a moment of weakness, he'd snitched a fat white-and-gold ceramic snowman from the centerpiece on the dining-room table and put it on his nightstand. If she'd noticed the piece was missing, she never said.

He didn't know quite how he felt about Allie's

Christmas onslaught. A little irritated at the takeover of his home. A bit amused by her almost frantic cheer. And something else—a wistful yearning he'd thought he'd given up as a boy.

Right now she sat on the living-room floor with Mrs. Vasquez, bags of spilled candy, red and green cellophane and shiny gold ribbon arrayed between them. They were making treat bags for every child attending the TaylorMade Christmas party tomorrow—nearly 150 at last reckoning.

As the tantalizing aroma of dinner wafted in from the kitchen, the two women worked together, counting foil-wrapped chocolates onto squares of cellophane. While one drew up the corners of the square into a neat packet, the other tied the ribbon around it.

In the half dozen or so years Mrs. Vasquez had worked for him, he'd asked nothing of her but to keep the house clean and cook dinner. But in the short time Allie had lived here, the two had bonded in the way women seemed to so easily. Thick as thieves, they'd chattered their way through decorating the house, baking tray after tray of Christmas cookies.

He'd have objected to the extra work Allie had given his housekeeper if Mrs. Vasquez hadn't been so obviously overjoyed with the new duties. He watched them now, giggling over the smallest thing, making a big show of stealing a chocolate, curling each ribbon with tender care.

The buzzer on the kitchen stove went off and Mrs. Vasquez sprang to her feet. "The casserole's done," she told Allie as she hurried off to the kitchen.

Smiling, Allie watched her go, then tipped her head up to Lucas. "Did you know she has twelve children? And nearly as many grandchildren?"

He shook his head. "We've never talked about it."

Allie's eyes widened in surprise. He felt a vague sense of failure. He'd employed the woman for so many years and knew next to nothing about her family. But until Allie, it hadn't seemed to matter.

Reaching into the bag of chocolates, she plucked one out and rose fluidly to her feet. "Did she tell you she's going back to the Philippines for a Christmas family reunion?"

"She said something about it." He vaguely remembered Mrs. Vasquez asking for an extra week off to visit family. But despite the woman's presence in his home nearly every day, it had never crossed his mind to probe any further.

A mysterious smile curving her lips, Allie unwrapped the chocolate in her hand, raised it to his lips. Reflexively, he opened his mouth, let her slip it inside. Her fingers brushing against his lips set off a heat that should have melted the sweet candy in seconds.

His gaze locked with hers, he felt tension sizzle between them, a sensual electricity that coursed through his body. He wanted to kiss her, to share the chocolate's dark rich flavor with her, to taste it mingling with her own unique essence. Keeping her vivid green eyes on him, her lips parted and she swayed slightly so that he reached out to her. Her soft emerald chenille sweater felt lush beneath his hand, warmed as it was by her skin.

Since that night she'd shared his bed, they'd resumed their wary dance, keeping their distance, touching only if necessary. But there were moments, many moments, when the connection between them was so real it was nearly tangible. Lucas knew it was only a matter of time before the attraction between them exploded again.

"Dinner is ready," Mrs. Vasquez called from the kitchen. As she returned to the living room, Lucas took a step back, shoving his hands into his pockets. Mrs. Vasquez pulled off her apron, dried her hands on it. "I'm afraid I have to go."

"No problem. I'm nearly done."

Allie waited until Mrs. Vasquez left, then lowered herself to the floor again and meticulously began counting out piles of the foil-wrapped candies. Carefully cutting a shiny square of red cellophane, she dropped a handful of chocolates onto it. Gathering up the corners, she struggled to hold it together while tying the ribbon.

Lucas went down on one knee beside her. "Let me help." He took the tiny packet, his fingers seeming too large for it. They got in the way of the gold ribbon and Allie laughed as she untangled a loop from his thumb. Seeing that ebullience on her flushed face, his heart lurched and he ached to draw her into his arms.

How was he ever going to let her go? As he sat back on his heels, the sense of imminent loss slammed into him. What had seemed a calculated business decision—a temporary marriage—now seemed terribly wrong, incredibly stupid.

And the end could come sooner than he'd originally thought. They'd sailed through the home visitation. And yesterday, John had notified Lucas he'd located a pregnant unwed teen planning to put her baby up for adoption. Due in January, the young girl was deciding between him and Allie and another couple. She would make her decision by the end of the year.

He hadn't told Allie yet. There was no reason to keep the information from her. But knowing it would be the beginning of the end, he couldn't quite force the words from his throat.

Counting out another pile of chocolates, she lifted the packet and again handed it to him. Her bright smile faded when she saw his face. "Lucas, what is it?"

He kept his focus on the party favor in his hands. "Everything else ready for tomorrow night?"

He could feel her gaze on him. "Helen organized a group of volunteers to wrap the presents tonight. Randy has a crew putting the finishing touches on the decorations."

"Good. You've done a great job with this." He moved to rise to his feet.

Allie put out a hand to stop him. "Lucas."

Her fingers lay featherlight on the back of his wrist. He wanted to clasp them to his heart, hold them there forever. "Yes?"

She chewed at her lower lip, the action both enticing and endearing. "Lucas, I…"

She looked away and Lucas had the sense she'd lost her nerve. Intuition tingled up his spine, setting him on alert. "What is it?"

She shook her head. "Nothing. Never mind."

He would have pressured her, but he had a secret of his own. Why push her to reveal something when he wasn't ready to be completely honest himself?

He straightened, held out his hand to her. "Let's get dinner. We can finish this later."

Helping her up, he walked with her into the kitchen, fingers locked with his. Sharing dinner with her was just one more pleasure he would sacrifice when he let her go.

But not yet. She was still his for now.

* * *

Dressed in a red felt elf suit, Allie supervised the impatient line of children waiting for Santa, her ears ringing with the almost mind-numbing noise in the TaylorMade cafeteria. Employees roamed the busy space, some of them costumed as elves or reindeer, entertaining the children or soothing the occasional tears. The TaylorMade staff boasted some surprising talents, from the two software engineers skilled at balloon animals to the VP of marketing's deft hand at magic.

Shifting to relieve her sore feet, Allie smiled at the next child in the queue for Santa. Helen, doubling as Mrs. Claus, had taken a well-deserved break, leaving Allie to monitor the Santa station. It was a delight to see the children's wide-eyed wonder, their joy as they accepted the gift set aside just for them.

Two hours into TaylorMade's First Annual Children's Christmas Party, it was clear the endeavor was a smashing success. From toddlers to midteens, kids filled the room, wolfing down pizza and soda, overindulging in candy and cake. Christmas carols blared from a music system brought in by one of the employees and Santa had a full slate of petitioners.

It had been Lucas's idea to corral the older teens to help with the party. When they'd first arrived, the teens had huddled together in a corner, eyeing each other and the adults in the room warily, casting disdainful glances at the younger children.

Lucas had sized up the situation instantly. He'd approached them matter-of-factly and within minutes had them organized into teams—one group to serve, another to assist at the crafts table, another to clean up. After a half hour he rotated the groups, making sure each had time simply to enjoy the party.

Of course he'd known instinctively what to do. He'd been one of those teens, lost in the foster system with no hope of adoption. Allie gained another bit of insight into her husband that evening.

She watched him now as he sat at the crafts table with a girl of five or six in his lap. His hands dwarfed the child's as he helped her glue ribbon around a foam ball. When the girl finished her ornament with a shower of glitter and got more of the sparkly stuff on Lucas than the ball, he just brushed the excess off his hands, unconcerned about the mess.

One of the teen helpers put the ornament in a paper sack for safekeeping, then the little girl hopped off Lucas's lap and raced for the food table. As if she'd been waiting her turn, another youngster held out her arms to Lucas to be lifted into his lap. He pulled her up without hesitation, giving her a brief hug as she settled into place.

As Allie bent to coax a balky three-year-old boy up to Santa, tears teased her eyes. The doubts she'd harbored about Lucas's ability to nurture a child had fled tonight. In the two hours she'd watched him at the party, he'd handled teenage pride and preschool needs with equal ease. The school-age kids trailed after him everywhere, hero worship shining in their eyes.

He might approach the children with a businessman's efficiency, but it was clear his heart led the way. And Allie would bet a month's salary he didn't even realize it.

Without volition, her hand went to her abdomen where Lucas's child had taken root. He deserved to know about this life the two of them had created. Although she'd planned to put off telling him until Christmas, she resolved to tell him that night after the party.

After seeing how comfortable he was with the children here, she was sure he would welcome her news.

Tiredness seeping into her, Allie smiled with gratitude as Helen moved across the room toward her. "Just in time," Allie said as the older woman took up her post next to Santa. "My feet were just about to give out."

"Go spend some time with that husband of yours." Helen nodded toward Lucas. "He looks like he could use a break, too."

Making her way through the crowd of children, Allie headed for the crafts table where Lucas was just helping another little girl from his lap. He caught sight of Allie as she closed the distance between them, his gray gaze intent as he watched her.

"How about some time off for good behavior?" She held her hand out to him.

Enclosing her hand in his, he rose from the table. He pressed a kiss to the back of her hand, then led her through the throng to the exit.

As they stepped outside, the frosty December air crept up the back of Lucas's neck, seeped through the sleeves of his wool sweater. Beside him, Allie shivered, the thin felt of her costume obviously providing no protection against the winter chill.

Taking hold of her shoulders, he turned her toward him. "Too cold? Should we go back inside?"

"In a minute," she said, wrapping her arms around herself.

He reached for her, pulled her close. "Here." He imagined his heat soaking into her, enfolding her. Her unique scent clung to her hair, a mix of wildflowers and an intangible female essence.

She sighed, her shivers easing as she relaxed. "You've been so wonderful tonight." She tipped her head back to look up at him. "You're so good with kids."

Joy at her compliment leapt in him, disbelief snapping at its heels. "I don't even know what I'm doing. Half the time I just guess."

She laughed. "Just like any other parent would."

"I'm not a parent."

"But you will be. Soon."

She had no idea how soon. He glanced away, looking out over the TaylorMade campus, toward the pond where a mist gathered. Then he forced his gaze back down at her. "About that…" he said slowly.

Panic flashed across her face. "You've changed your mind about wanting a child?"

Her alarm puzzled him, set off an unease in the pit of his stomach. "Why?"

"Because…I thought maybe…" For a moment she looked frantic, then she took a deep breath. "*Have* you changed your mind?"

"No! Of course not."

She squeezed her eyes shut; when she opened them, her relief was evident. "Good. That's good."

"What about you?" Raising his hand to her face, he stroked her cheek with his thumb. "Any second thoughts about adopting?"

She paused for one breath, two, before shaking her head slowly. Her hesitation chewed at him, made him uneasy.

"I heard from John." He locked his gaze with hers, tried to decipher the thoughts hidden behind them. "He may have found a baby for us." He told her about the expectant teenage girl, watching her face for a reaction.

She listened silently before asking, "When will John know?"

"Before New Year's. The girl promised to make a decision by then." He brought his other hand up to cup her face, wishing he could will her compliance with his touch. "If she chooses us, that means you only have another year or so."

"Not very long," she murmured. Was that relief he heard?

"No, it isn't." To him, it didn't seem long enough. He let his gaze wander across her face, settle on her lips. The urgency to kiss her, to claim her, took hold of him. "Allie…"

Her name hung in the air between them as he lowered his mouth to hers. He brushed his lips softly against hers at first, deepening the kiss by slow degrees, lightly tracing with his tongue before dipping briefly inside. She moaned at each gentle thrust, the audible sound of her pleasure combined with the wet heat of her mouth an intoxicating blend.

"Damn, I want you," he groaned. "I tell myself to keep away, but I can't seem to resist touching you."

"I want you to touch me. I want you to hold me."

He kissed her cheeks, along the bridge of her nose, the line of her jaw, every inch of her sweet and warm. "Then what, Allie? If we make love, what happens after that? When we have a year together, maybe less."

Stay with me! I won't let you go! The words exploded from deep inside him, shocking him with their vehemence. He bit them back to keep from saying them out loud.

She stroked his back, her touch maddening. "I don't know, Lucas. I just know I want you, too."

He drew back, his gaze on her, the promise in her

green eyes enough to burn him alive. His body clamored at him to take what she offered. Nobility had never been his strong suit and Allie seemed to strip away his decorum with ease.

"I didn't marry you for this, Allie," he said harshly. "Only for a child."

She winced a little at his bald statement, edged back from him far enough that his hands dropped to his sides. Her teeth caught her lower lip, worrying it. "There's something I have to tell you, Lucas."

Terror burst inside him. She wanted to leave him, to terminate their marriage! "About what?" He pushed the question past a throat gone raw with fear. "The adoption?"

The damned uncertainty flickered in her eyes again. "Yes and no."

He felt so tightly wound with tension, he thought he'd snap in two. "Tell me," he rasped out.

She glanced inside the brightly lit cafeteria where the party continued, the revelers oblivious to the turmoil brewing just outside. Her gaze met his again. "Not here. When we get home."

He ought to just ask her, straight out, if she was leaving him. Better to know right away than have the agony linger as it did with his mother, one alcohol-drenched day after the other. But he had only to look at Allie's determined face to know she wouldn't answer him.

"At home, then," he said, trying to push back the desolation inside him.

He took her hand and led her back into the cafeteria. He refused to leave her side for the rest of the evening, too afraid if he let her go physically it would just hasten her eventual desertion. When the children lined up at the end of the party to tell him goodbye, to give him a hug and a thank-you, he watched her out of the corner of his eye, tried to decode the expression on her face.

She seemed so happy when she spoke to the children, so eager to pull them into her arms. What could have made her change her mind about the adoption, about their marriage?

You'll know soon enough, he told himself grimly. As the room cleared out, foster parents coming to pick up their charges, the TaylorMade staff tidying up and heading home themselves, resignation weighed heavier and heavier on Lucas's shoulders.

Finally, it was time for him and Allie to leave. Slipping into the restroom, she changed quickly back into the heavy sweater and jeans she'd had on before the party. He held her hand as they walked to the Mercedes, wanting to keep the contact as long as possible. Their unfinished business dangled between them as he drove them home, twisting his gut into knots.

She remained silent as they pulled into the garage, as he helped her from the car, as they entered the house. Tossing his keys onto the breakfast table, he had to grit his teeth to keep from grabbing her shoulders, to shake the words from her.

He stood there in the breakfast room, watching her where she stood just inside the door to the garage, waiting for her cue. She wouldn't quite meet his gaze.

"Allie..." Her name seemed torn from his lips.

Raising her eyes to his at last, her teeth claimed her bottom lip again. "Lucas..." She glanced away. When she looked at him again, tears glimmered in her eyes. "I'm pregnant, Lucas. I'm going to have your baby."

Chapter Twelve

He looked like a man who'd been sucker punched. Even knowing in advance how difficult her news would be for him to take, Allie's stomach churned when she saw his reaction.

He seemed to struggle to breathe. "You're what?"

She crossed her arms over her middle. "I'm pregnant. With your baby."

"But how…" He shook his head, as if denying the truth. "It was only one time. You said you were safe."

Anger bubbled inside her at his accusatory tone. "I thought I was. It was just after my period. I shouldn't have been fertile."

He seemed to grow taller in his outrage. "But you damn well were!"

Turning his back, he paced away from her, out of sight into the living room. Shaking herself into action, she followed him. His long legs covered the length of the expansive living room in a few strides before he turned back toward her.

"This changes everything," he said, a frightening edge to his low voice. He stared down at the carpet, his hands closing into fists. His head swung up. "How the hell do we go through with the adoption if you're pregnant?"

She moved closer with tentative steps. "We still can, if that's what you want. But this child…" She touched her belly lightly. "He or she is yours, now. Without any red tape, without any home inspections or county approvals."

She stopped a few feet from him, tipped her head up to meet his gaze. "You wanted a child, Lucas. We were granted that miracle, in a way we didn't expect."

He reached for her, his hands gripping her arms. "But *my* child, Allie…" Looking away, he dragged a breath into his lungs before turning his intense gray gaze back to her. "My mother died an alcoholic. How do I know I haven't passed that same nightmare on to my child?"

Raising her hands to his face, she stroked his jaw soothingly. "We don't know. We can't. We can only do our best."

"My best…" His jaw worked. "My best damn well might not be enough."

"I'll be here, Lucas," she assured him. "As long as you want me."

She couldn't help herself. As much as she might try to hide it, she knew her love for him shone from her eyes, was written clearly across her face. He must see it.

For a moment, she saw recognition flash across his face, an instant of acceptance. But just as quickly, he denied what he'd seen, closing himself off to the possibility.

"As long as I want you," he said flatly. "For the child."

Allie could have wept. Dropping her hands, she looked away. "Yes. For the child."

"We'll have to change the marriage agreement."

At his thoughtful tone, she lifted her gaze back to his. Could it be he wanted to change their temporary arrangement to a permanent one?

With his next statement, he dashed all her hopes. "I assume you'll want visitation rights."

He might as well have ripped out her heart. This time she couldn't keep back the tears. "Of course," she forced out past a tight throat.

She tried to keep them at bay, but the tears spilled down her cheeks. Swiping at her face, she tried to brush them aside. "Sorry. I guess it's hormones."

He reached for her, took her into his arms. "Not your fault. None of this is your fault. I never should have lost control that morning."

"There were two in that bed. I could have said no."

He gazed down at her, the expression on his face so tender the tears filled her eyes again. He smoothed them away with the pads of his thumbs. "Don't cry." He pressed a kiss on each cheek. "Please don't."

Hope, never quite absent from her heart, struggled to life again. The softness in his face, the gentleness of his touch...she'd never seen Lucas so open, so giving. If there was any time to share her feelings with him, this was it.

"Lucas," she gasped out, then took a breath before she lost her courage. "About the agreement, the marriage." She swallowed back misgivings, doubts. "We don't have to separate. We can continue, make it a real marriage.''

His eyes narrowed. ''A real marriage?''

''Stay together.'' She clutched at his arms, tried to transmit her conviction by the contact. ''Make a family, Lucas. You and me and the baby. Be husband and wife for—''

''Forever?'' A veil seemed to drop over his face as he tugged his arms from her grasp. ''Forever's a myth, Allie.''

A cold knot gripped her middle. ''No.'' She shook her head. ''It's not.''

''I suppose you love me.'' His hard tone slashed through her like a razor. ''That you can't live without me?''

Yes! she wanted to scream. *I love you!* But stone by stone, he'd retreated behind his walls again. She knew he would reject her pronouncement, no matter how passionately she stated it.

Stubborn determination settled inside her. ''I want to stay married, Lucas. For the baby, for a family—pick the reason you'll accept. If I say I love you—''

''Don't,'' he rasped out. ''I won't have you telling me that.''

Bleakness settled around her, colder than the tule fog that curled in the darkness outside. ''It doesn't matter,'' she said bitterly. ''But this baby deserves both a mother and a father.''

''And if we'd adopted?'' His gray gaze seemed to pierce her heart, lay her bare. ''Would you have walked away?''

Tipping up her chin, she kept her eyes on him. ''No. Before now, I might have thought I could, but now I know…I never could have walked away.''

Silence stretched between them, interminable and as sharp-edged as broken glass. When he spoke, his chill tone sent a shudder through her. "This isn't what we agreed to, Allie." His fists clenched as if he battled something inside him, an enemy he barely kept at bay. Then he nodded abruptly. "We'll stay married. As long as you like. As long as you understand love has no part in our relationship."

A sadness swept over her. "But our child...you'll love our baby, won't you?"

She expected more anger. Instead he stared at her, stunned. "I don't think—" He looked out the living-room window as if searching for an answer in the fog-bound night.

"Don't think?" she prompted quietly.

The confession came out as a raw whisper. "I don't know how, Allie. I wish I could say I did. I wish I could—" He squeezed his eyes shut, his throat working. "Too many years, Allie. Too much loneliness. I never learned how. Or if I did, life wrenched it out of me."

Her heart constricted in her chest. "But the child you wanted to adopt...how could you..." *How could you dare adopt a child you couldn't love?* The unspoken words hung between them.

His gaze locked with hers, and she saw the agony, the doubts in those turbulent gray eyes. "I thought it wouldn't matter. That I could give a child other things...food and shelter, the finest education..." He dragged in a breath. "That's enough, isn't it?"

His troubled gaze pleaded with her to tell him yes. And perhaps it would be enough if he could be as kind to his son or daughter as he had been to the children tonight. But how could a child thrive without a father's love?

Uncertainty a weight in her chest, she forced herself to smile up at him. When she gently stroked his rough cheek, the harsh line of his jaw eased, the tension in his brow relaxed. He reached out, curved his hand around the back of her neck.

He rested his brow against hers. "You can love enough for both of us," he whispered. He kissed her, then moved past her to climb the stairs two at a time.

Her breath hitching on a sob, Allie switched off the lights and followed him up the stairs. In her room, she stood by her bed, one hand caressing her belly. Her gaze fixed on the door leading to the nursery and without thought, she crossed the room to open the door.

Her hand trembled as she turned the knob. She hadn't stepped into this room since that first day. Now she felt compelled to look inside, as if by seeing it, her baby would become more real, less a dream.

Fumbling for the light, she flipped it on, squinted against the glare. Nothing had changed since she'd last seen the room. The mobile still dangled from the ceiling, the woebegone bear still hunched in a corner of the crib. The drab walls still needed some bright decoration to liven them, something to catch a baby's eye.

With a sigh, she moved across the room, skimmed her hand across the top of the changing table, let her fingers drift over the smooth wood of the dresser. She noticed the top dresser drawer was slightly ajar and she wondered if Lucas had already started filling it with baby things.

Tugging open the drawer, she peeked inside, expecting to see tiny folded shirts and onesies. But only a rumpled piece of paper lay inside the otherwise empty drawer. She drew it out, realizing an instant before she turned it over what it was.

The picture of Lucas's mother, the one Teresa had given her, the one Lucas had torn from the Thanksgiving book. He hadn't thrown it away, had instead tucked it into the baby's dresser. Had he intended to show it to his child one day, tell him or her, this is your grandmother?

Smoothing the sheet of paper, Allie looked for Lucas in the woman's face. The gray eyes were familiar, but the smile—Lucas smiled so seldom. His mother had been happy, at least at some time in her life. She'd apparently given so little to Lucas—had she given even a scrap of this happiness to her son?

Carefully setting the paper back inside as she'd found it, Allie closed the drawer and left the room. She'd gotten from Lucas what she'd ached for—a permanent life with him. But could she bear to live that life when the love between them was only from her to him?

She could and she would for their child. Lucas had said she would love their baby enough for both of them; she would have to love Lucas enough for them both, as well. She would always hope that someday, his heart would open to her, but if it never did, she would eke out of their marriage whatever happiness she could.

Undressing quickly for bed, she performed her nightly routine by rote, then crawled tiredly under the covers. With the light off, she lay in the darkness, focusing on the child growing within her.

She barely heard his knock, as if he didn't want to wake her if she'd already fallen asleep. Flipping the light back on, she called out, ''Yes?''

After a moment's hesitation, he stepped into her room. He wore pajama bottoms, his muscled chest enticing in the dim light. He stared at her in the bed, his gray eyes intense.

"Can I stay with you tonight, Allie?"

That he'd asked, that he waited for her answer meant more to her in that moment than a profession of love. Shifting to one side, she pulled the blankets back for him. "Stay with me," she murmured.

He switched off the light then climbed in beside her, his warmth a pleasant shock. Pulling her up against him, he buried his face in her hair, brushed his lips across her brow. His arms wrapped around her, he made no move that could be considered sexual. He just held her, his arm draped around her waist, his hand resting lightly on her belly.

She wondered if she would ever understand this man. Drifting off to sleep, the puzzle of him tangled in her dreams, teasing her to solve it.

Allie pulled the Volvo in next to Lucas's Mercedes in the garage, still warmed by her family's Christmas-day celebration. Her initial disappointment when Lucas refused to go with her had faded with the first hugs and joyful greetings of her siblings, her nieces and nephews. Now, as she shut off the engine and shut her eyes, she basked in the sweet joy of the day.

With a sigh, she grabbed her purse and the plate of cookies Sherril had insisted she take to Lucas, and climbed from the car. She considered bringing in the presents from her family, as well, then decided they could stay in the trunk until tomorrow. She was eager to see Lucas, anxious to see his reaction to the gift she had tucked away in the fragrant branches of their Christmas tree.

She slipped inside the house, set down purse and cookies on the breakfast-nook table. A plate and glass sat on the kitchen counter by the sink and Allie's heart ached at the thought of Lucas's lonely Christmas dinner.

He had insisted a crucial deadline prevented him from joining her at Sherril's, but Allie understood the real reason. She'd seen the emotions warring in his eyes. Even as he yearned to be part of the festivities, Lucas feared being the outsider, always on the periphery of the loving circle of her family.

So she hadn't pushed, despite her disappointment. And now she bubbled with excitement, anticipating his pleasure at opening her present to him. She'd picked it up a week ago and it had been all she could do to wait until Christmas day to give it to him.

She peeked into the living room, saw his laptop open on the coffee table, but no Lucas. Taking the stairs two at a time, she checked his bedroom. The bedside lamp illuminated the empty room, the neatly made bed.

Back downstairs, she went through the kitchen, peered out the French doors leading to the back deck. The fog-shrouded moon cast its feeble light on a solitary figure hunched in a redwood chair. Allie stared at him a long moment before hurrying to the living room to pluck a small gold-foil-wrapped box from its hiding place in the tree.

She eased open the French door, the intense winter chill frosting her cheeks. "Lucas?"

She could barely make out his face in the darkness. "Did you have a good time?" His quiet words seemed to drift toward her like the curls of mist on the back lawn.

"It was wonderful." Crossing the deck, she dragged a chair closer and sat beside him, his gift in her lap. "Sherril and Stephen's kids performed a Christmas skit that had us all in stitches. Dinner was incredible—I made a complete pig of myself. Then after dinner we got out the old family videos. The kids got such a kick out of seeing the goofy clothes their parents used to wear."

She took his hand, closed it in both of hers. If only she could transfer her joy of the day to him with the contact. "I wish you could have been there."

"It sounds like you enjoyed the day without me."

Unease rippled through her at the edge to his tone. "It would have been better with you."

His tension translated itself into the broad hand that nestled between her own. Then he sighed, pulled her hand to his lips, pressed a kiss into her palm. "Damn, I missed you."

She leaned closer to him, rested her head on his shoulder. Then she remembered his gift. She picked it up, held it out to him. "Merry Christmas."

Releasing her hand, he took the small, gold box. "What is this?"

"Your Christmas present." She grinned, nearly giddy with excitement. "Go ahead. Open it."

Feeling like the world's biggest idiot, Lucas stared down at the neatly wrapped box in his hand. "I didn't get you anything."

If she was disappointed, she hid it well. "You didn't need to. I wanted to get you this."

Lucas turned the box over and over in his hands. For

most of his life, Christmas had passed like any other day. Despite the modest gifts from the Calderas over the years, he'd refused to give meaning to the holiday.

It hadn't crossed his mind to buy something for Allie, although it should have. It had been all too clear these past few weeks how important Christmas was to Allie.

And now she'd given him something and he had nothing to offer her in return. He felt the urge to return the gold foil box to her, but he had only to look at her shy, expectant smile to know that would hurt her far more than having nothing with which to reciprocate.

Under her watchful gaze, he tore off the paper. Whatever was inside the box, surely he could muster a convincing thank-you. She didn't have to know how overwhelmed he felt at her gift.

Then he opened the box, saw the heavy gold ring. His initials figured in platinum, tiny diamonds studding the loops of the *L.* My God, how could she have known?

"Look inside," she said softly.

He pulled the shining gold ring from the blue velvet box, held it up to the faint light from the kitchen. He could just make out the words, *With love from Allie,* carved inside. Emotions swamped him, and his hands shook as he carefully replaced the ring in the box.

"I asked John," she said, answering his silent question. She touched the precious thing with a fingertip. "He told me you'd always wanted a ring like this."

How had John known? Lucas supposed there had been enough times in college when he and John had wandered through Berkeley together or gone into San Francisco for the day. Lucas hadn't realized his hungry stares into jewelry-store windows had been so obvious.

A custom-made ring, created just for him, would symbolize his arrival in a world that didn't want him.

He'd long ago dismissed the idea as a bit of vanity he didn't need. Yet holding it now, the soft glow of gold and wink of diamonds brought the old longings, the old hurts sharply to the surface.

He glanced over at Allie, at her sweet upturned face. Watching her, it was as if a chasm yawned between them. He would be safe on his own side, safe and alone. To reach Allie, he would have to leap over his fears, the old remembered pain. That vault would tear away every crutch, all his walls and barriers.

He only had to say, *thank you.*

But even that shred of gratitude froze in his throat. God help him, cowardice gripped his heart like a fist, forced him back behind his walls.

"Take it back." The mean-spirited words leapt from his mouth before he could stop them. He shut the ring box with a snap and shoved it into her hands. "I don't want it."

Her eyes went wide with the beginnings of hurt. "But John said—"

"I don't give a damn what John said." He rose abruptly, knocking the chair backward. "I don't want it." Not even understanding what drove him, he headed for the house.

"Lucas!"

Her cry struck him between the shoulder blades with the force of a dagger. He staggered a step, then continued inside.

She was right behind him. She grabbed his sleeve, turned him around with the force of her will. "I know the world hurt you," she hissed. "I know there's more pain inside you than I can even imagine. But to be so cruel…''

She took a breath, the sound edging on tears. Snatching up his hand, she stuffed the box into it. ''Take it. Even if it hurts you. Even if it means nothing to you. Take it.'' She dragged in another breath. ''Because *I* gave it to you. Because it means something to *me*.''

She pushed past him then, raced upstairs. He stood there, feeling lower than low, like the worst kind of vermin.

She was his wife, the mother of his child. How could he have treated her so shabbily? Good God, what was wrong with him?

He sagged into a kitchen chair, the box clutched in his hand. He didn't deserve the gift. He didn't deserve Allie.

Unable to help himself, he opened the box again, pulled the ring from it. And in the pale kitchen light, he read over and over again the inscription inside.

Chapter Thirteen

Lucas stood just outside the doorway of the TaylorMade cafeteria, his gaze fixed across the room on a table crowded with employees. Allie sat among them, Helen on her left and engineer Randy Sato on her right. The weak sunshine of early January filtered through the windows as the staff enjoyed an afternoon coffee break.

Rather than enter the cafeteria and join them, Lucas hung back, not wanting them to see him. His presence tended to throw a damper on staff gatherings. Even more so since Allie's announcement about her pregnancy.

Allie's revelation, coupled with their commitment to continue the marriage, had roused in Lucas a protectiveness and possessiveness so fierce it frightened him. Even the most innocuous look from another man brought up an almost caveman response to declare his ownership. Bone-deep and primitive, the urgency to make clear his claim on her shook him even more than the passion she never failed to stir in him.

After the mess he had made of Christmas, it had taken until now, the first week of January, for Allie to speak to him beyond what was strictly required. When John had informed him shortly after Christmas that the pregnant teen had changed her mind about adopting, Lucas had tried to draw Allie into a discussion about whether they should still try to adopt. He'd barely gotten a word out of her and the issue remained unresolved. She still refused to share his bed with him. No more than he deserved since he had hurt her so deeply when he'd spurned her gift.

He'd tried to make amends with a diamond necklace his jeweler had quickly put together for him. But although she had responded politely to the present and had put it on at his prompting, he hadn't seen her wear it since.

Even as her belly swelled with their child, his passion for her grew daily. Sometimes he ached for her so badly his body shook with the pent-up fire of his attraction to her. Being so close to her yet holding back was an agony, one that set him so much on edge he thought he'd go mad.

The day he had to fight down the impulse to take a swing at Randy Sato because Allie had smiled down the conference table at him at a meeting, Lucas knew he was in bad shape. But he couldn't seem to stop the pang inside him when he saw how easily she interacted with her fellow employees. She related to them with an effortlessness he had never possessed.

The staff respected him, although some of them he intimidated. But they never joked with him, never stopped him in the hallway for a bit of chitchat as they did with Allie. In the years he'd owned TaylorMade, even at the beginning when they'd operated on a shoestring, he'd never encouraged the kind of socializing that seemed to come so naturally to Allie.

He'd always considered personal lives irrelevant in the workplace. But watching Allie, it hit home that his employees spent a good chunk of their lives at TaylorMade. It made perfect sense they would strive to connect with each other.

Until now it had never bothered him to be set apart from the others. He was the boss; it was expected that he be somewhat isolated from the staff. But the staff seemed truly delighted with Allie's company. The way she seemed to have forged such strong bonds with the other employees, Lucas for the first time felt like the outsider in the one place he'd thought he belonged. Like that child that had yearned for so long for stability, for a friend, a connection, he felt cut off from the camaraderie.

As he watched, Allie threw back her head in laughter, exuberance in the sound. But when he caught her eye across the room, her happiness seemed to dim. Her wary expression wrenched something inside him, gave him a sense of loss he didn't understand. She pressed her hands to the table as if to rise; he motioned her to stay put.

She kept her gaze on him as he remained in the doorway. She looked flustered and unsure, as if she suspected he wanted something of her, but couldn't decipher it. If he could have spoken to her, he would have confessed he hadn't a clue either, other than wanting to hold her, to protect her, to find a way to her heart.

She looked his way again, and this time said her goodbyes and gathered up her jacket. As she approached him, her serious expression told him nothing of what she was feeling. Only her green eyes revealed the turbulence inside her.

"Was there something you needed, Lucas?" she asked, her cool tone uncharacteristic.

He had to find a way to get her back. Impulsively, he took her hand. "Come walk with me."

Her eyes narrowed at his demand, but she nodded in acquiescence. He helped her on with her coat, then reclaimed her hand, leading her from the building and out into the weak winter sunshine.

As they headed for the pond, the rain-laden grass gave under their feet, squishing with each step. Lucas kept a firm hand on Allie's elbow, catching her when she slipped a little on the slick surface.

They stopped at a stone bench at the pond's edge. Allie lowered herself onto the bench and Lucas sat beside her. She gazed out over the pond, tracing the path of the swans as they crossed the still water.

He knew she was waiting for him to speak. Words danced in his mind in a confusing chaos, refusing to fall into any ordered pattern. Squeezing his eyes shut, he shook his head, then plunged in. "Allie, I'm sorry."

Allie could see the regret in his hooded gaze, heard the sincerity in his voice. But he'd hurt her at Christmas, wounded her badly. And even though she loved the man more than she ought to, she didn't feel particularly inclined right then to make things easy for him.

She cast him a skeptical look. "So you've said before. But somehow we always end up back with this distance between us."

She could see that stung and felt a moment of remorse. But she held her tongue, leaving it to him to talk. "I've made mistakes," he said. "I'm no good at relationships. I never learned how to do it right."

"Nice excuse, Lucas. But you can't keep blaming your past for the mess you've made of the present."

Anger flared in his gray eyes and she thought she'd pushed him too far. Yet as he regained his composure, she wondered if it would have been better for him to explode, to burn away his restraint.

His jaw tightening, he turned toward her, took her hands in his. "Allie, thank you for the Christmas gift. Thank you for caring enough to have it made for me."

Her gaze fell to his hands, noticed the ring for the first time on his right pinky. "You're wearing it."

"I put it on this morning. I don't intend to take it off."

Her feelings for him welled up inside her, flowing from her heart, filling her. She could no more hold back the words shaping her emotions than she could resist taking another breath. "Lucas." She laid her hand against his cheek. "I love you, Lucas."

He seemed startled and she could see the now-familiar instinct to escape in his eyes. Curling her fingers around his neck, she gave a gentle squeeze. "I love you and there's no avoiding it. You can't change the way I feel, no matter what, so there's no point in running away from it."

He cupped his hand over hers, held her there. "I care for you, Allie. I cherish you. I want to call that feeling love...." He looked away from her, out across the pond, to some distant point beyond. Then he focused on her again, intent. "But I can't lie to you. I know love is more, greater."

He brought her hand to his lips, shut his eyes. "There's a lock on my heart, Allie. Too many years of a mother more in love with a bottle than her own son, too many homes where I was unwelcome."

Even as tears closed Allie's throat, her love spilled from her. "You're always welcome in my heart, Lucas."

His gaze locked with hers. "If I had the key, I would give it to you. I would open to you...to our child. But I don't..."

He pulled her to him then, clutching her close. His heart thudded in a rapid beat, his breathing dragged in and out of his lungs raggedly. "You'll never want for anything, Allie, you or our child. As long as you're with me. Every part of me there is to give is yours."

Except his love. She wept inside at the realization. But at least they'd broken down the walls again and perhaps they could build a new bridge between them.

When Lucas eased away from her and rose, his smile tugged at her heart. "What do you say we leave work early? Go to a movie and dinner."

She nodded, too overwhelmed to speak. This would be enough, wouldn't it? A generous man, giving her whatever she desired? It was close to love.

It would have to be enough.

Late that night, after a wonderful film and an even better dinner at an upscale Italian restaurant, Allie walked with Lucas into the house, sated and content. When Lucas came up behind her, slipping her jacket from her shoulders and pressing a kiss to the back of her neck, the sizzling attraction between them flared immediately into white-hot heat. He'd held back every night, until she felt crazy with wanting him. But she sensed tonight he wouldn't stop at holding her in his arms in bed. And she was willing to go as far as he would take her.

As Lucas hung up their jackets in the coat closet, Allie's gaze fell on the answering machine's flashing red light. In spite of her warm contentment, a shiver of premonition arced up her spine. She hit the play button and waited while the tape rewound, trying to shake off her dread.

"Allie, call me!" her sister said, panic obvious in her tone. "As soon as you get home, no matter what time!"

Lucas laid his hand on the back of neck, lightly stroked the sudden tension there. "What is it?"

Her hands shook as she dialed her sister's number. "I don't know."

Please, don't let it be the baby, she prayed. *Or Danny or Lisa.*

"Sherril," she gasped out when her sister answered the phone. "It's me."

Sherril sucked in a breath and Allie could hear her tears. "It's Dad," she said. "He's wandered away from the care home. They can't find him."

Terror gripped Allie as she set down the phone. It was the dead of winter, even colder in Reno than Sacramento. For her father to be out wandering the streets…

Lucas turned her toward him. "Allie, what's wrong?"

Her mind raced as she tried to figure out what to do next. "My dad…they don't know where he is."

"Who doesn't?" He shook her gently. "You're not making sense."

She raised her gaze to his. "I have to leave. I have to go to Reno, now, tonight."

His hands tightened on her shoulders. "Allie, I still don't understand. Why are you going to Reno?"

She tried to shrug away from him, gave up when he refused to loosen his grip. "To find my father. He left the home. They haven't been able to find him." Pulling harder, she finally broke free. "I have to leave."

Lucas followed right behind her as she hurried up the stairs. "Then I'm going with you."

Behind Lucas's arrogant tone, Allie sensed a trace of fear. But she had her father to think about. Lucas would have to deal with his own emotions.

In her room, she went straight to her dresser, pulled out a handful of underwear, bras, socks. "No, Lucas. Please, I just have to do this by myself."

"Allie, I want to be with you." He dogged her steps as she crossed to the closet, tugged out jeans and sweaters. "I want to help you."

"No!" She clutched the clothes to her chest. She wasn't being fair to him, but panic had stripped her of compassion. She just shook her head, pushed past him.

"How long will you be gone? Can you at least tell me that?"

"I don't know!" She dumped the clothes on the bed, fighting back tears as she returned to the closet for her suitcase. "As long as it takes to find him."

He reached for her, tried to grab her shoulder. "Take me with you." A pleading note had crept into his voice.

She evaded his grasp. "I can't, Lucas. Please understand—"

"I don't understand anything!" He dragged in a

breath and his voice dropped to a harsh whisper. "Just that you're leaving. You won't let me help."

"Oh, Lucas." Dropping the suitcase to the floor, she took his hands. "My father…he…" *Has Alzheimer's,* she tried to force herself to say. But it still felt like too great a betrayal to her father to tell Lucas.

"He's very sick, and he's missing. He needs me, Lucas. My family needs me."

He squeezed her hands. "Then let me be what *you* need. Let me in, Allie."

Crazy with worry, she couldn't hold back the anger that surged up in her. "Let you in…" She bit out the words. "When you refuse to open up to me, when you keep your heart under lock and key…"

Her hand flew to her mouth as the cruel words hung between them. "I'm sorry, Lucas."

He released her hands, took a step back. "Why apologize? It's only the truth." He moved toward the door. "You'd better get going."

She closed the distance between them, took his hand. "I love you, Lucas. That hasn't changed. But I have to see to my father."

He wouldn't meet her gaze. He just nodded, tugged his hand from hers. She knew she had to somehow make things right between them again, but it would have to wait until her father was safe.

She threw her clothes into the suitcase, grabbed up what necessities she could think of from the bathroom and added them to the pile. If she needed anything else, she could buy it in Reno.

Snapping the suitcase shut, she turned to Lucas. He'd shut himself off to her again and her dreams of an intimate connection with him were shattered. Would it always be like this with him, one step forward, two back?

"I'll call when I get to Reno, let you know where I'm staying."

She bent to pick up the suitcase, but with a stubborn set to his jaw, he took it from her, carried it from her room. "I'll wait for your call."

"You don't have to wait up. I can leave a message."

"I'll wait."

At the bottom of the stairs, she tried again to reach him. "I shouldn't be gone long. At least I hope..." She didn't want to think about how many days her father could survive exposed to a Reno winter.

"Take as long as you need." He wouldn't look at her as he strode toward the door to the garage.

Snatching up her purse, she hurried after him. In the garage, he hefted the suitcase into the trunk of the Volvo, slammed the lid shut. Then he opened the car door for her, helped her inside.

His hand lingered on her arm and she wondered if he would lean in and kiss her goodbye. But although his gaze dropped to her lips, he straightened abruptly and backed away.

Allie closed the car door, then started the engine so she could roll down the electric window. "Lucas."

He had turned his back to activate the automatic garage door. When she called his name a second time, he turned toward her, his body stiff with reluctance.

"You know I'll be back," she said firmly, keeping her gaze locked with his.

A softness flickered briefly in his face, a trace of hope. He reached through the window to brush her cheek with his thumb. He looked so lost, like a boy who'd faced too many broken promises. "Find your father, Allie."

Then he turned away, and disappeared inside the house. Filled with misgivings, Allie backed from the garage and set out for Reno.

The instant he stepped inside the house, Lucas strode to the living-room window and watched the Volvo's taillights retreat into the darkness. A red-hot poker in his gut wouldn't have been as painful as seeing her leave. And although his rational mind told him she would be back, he couldn't seem to hold back the fear that swamped him in waves.

It was ridiculous to compare Allie to his mother. There was no logic to it.

Even so, all his childhood insecurities seemed to close in, wrapping ropes of pain around his heart. As a boy, he'd never been able to banish the uneasy certainty that something he'd done or some vital quality he'd lacked had driven his mother away. As an adult, he could refute that childish conviction with an adult's reasoning. But all it took was Allie's leaving to bring it all back.

Agitated, he crossed the room to the sofa and sank onto it, dropping his head into his hands. How many times had he driven Allie away, with words, with actions? Too many to count. And yet she still professed to love him, still made her way back to him again and again.

What if this was her breaking point? She'd left to see to her father, her family. Surely her commitment to family was a stronger hold for her than the short-lived love she said she felt for him. *You keep your heart under lock and key,* she'd said. How could any woman persevere with a man who couldn't love her?

Dear God, what if she left him for good? What if by being away from him a few days, she saw more clearly he wasn't worth the trouble? His mother had certainly said it enough times... *Lucas, I swear you're more trouble than you're worth.* More often than not, she'd made the pronouncement between one drink and the next. But he'd always wondered, if he'd tried harder, could he have kept her from taking that drink?

He shook his head, trying to drive away the doubts. That was his past talking. This was Allie, not his ruined, weak-willed mother. If Allie said she loved him, surely there would be enough strength to that emotion to bring her back.

Moving slowly, feeling a hundred years old, Lucas slipped off his shoes, stretched out on the sofa. He considered going upstairs to his room. But what if he fell asleep, missed her call? He craved hearing her voice again.

At the thought of sleeping alone in his bed, despair bloomed inside him. He would stay here and a part of him would pretend Allie was on her way back to him, on her way home.

He shut his eyes against the pain, then opened them again when sleep lapped at him, threatening to pull him under. He had to stay awake, had to wait for her. But the turmoil of emotions had exhausted him, dragging him into unconsciousness. He descended immediately into nightmare, horrifying dreams of Allie moving faster and further from him, always out of reach. It wasn't until the last ring of the telephone before the answering machine picked up that he woke.

He lay there, dazed, as the beep sounded and Allie's voice came on. "Lucas? Are you there?"

A pause while she waited for him to answer. He remained on the sofa, immobilized by fear. If he lifted up the phone, if he talked to her, she might say goodbye. But she wouldn't leave a message like that on the answering machine.

A long sigh, then she continued, "We're at the Best Western in Reno. The number is..."

Another hesitation as she searched for the phone number, then she read the digits to him. "Lucas, I..."

He could hear the tears in her voice, could hear her need for him. He scrambled up off the sofa, hurried for the phone.

"I'll talk to you later," she said breathlessly, just as he laid his hand on the receiver.

"Allie?"

A click and the dial tone as she hung up. Trembling, Lucas rewound the message, scribbled the phone number on a scrap of paper. His hand poised over the buttons of the phone, he hesitated.

Was he calling her back because she needed him? Or because he needed her? How could he add to her worry for her father with his selfishness? She had to focus on her family now, not him.

But he did need her, desperately. He set aside the phone, let the silence of the empty house close in on him. He needed her here to tell him again she loved him, to reassure him there was something in him worth loving.

Rewinding the message, he listened to it again, absorbing every nuance of her voice, focusing on each word. Yet as much as he searched for her love in the short message, somehow he only heard goodbye.

Chapter Fourteen

Slumped in her chair next to her father's hospital bed, Allie tried to gather enough energy to go into the bathroom to wash her face and brush her hair. But she felt so weary, even the few steps to the bathroom seemed too far to walk.

She'd urged her sister and brother to return to the hotel sometime around three in the morning to get some sleep and call their spouses back home. Allie had managed a fitful night's rest in the unwelcoming plastic hospital chair and greeted the day feeling stiff and sore.

Even as the steady rise and fall of her father's chest reassured her, her heart ached with loneliness and an unrelenting yearning to see her own husband. In the week since her father had wandered away from the care home until now, his fourth day in the hospital since being found, she had spoken to Lucas only a handful of times. Each time Lucas had barely said a word, letting her do all the talking.

She supposed she should be grateful; she'd needed the chance to pour out her fears, the guilt she couldn't seem to put aside. But something about Lucas's brittle silence nagged at her.

Even his anger would have been more welcome. With anger, she at least knew how he felt. By withdrawing, he left her to guess at the emotions inside him. She feared he'd locked himself up tight again as if he no longer trusted himself to feel.

God, she wished he was here. Fighting back tears, Allie shifted in her chair, fixed her gaze on her father's frail form under the neat hospital sheet. Maybe she should have had him come with her. She could have leaned on him, let him help her through the long, terrifying nights worrying about her father.

She had to admit now it wasn't just her desire to protect French's privacy that led her to reject Lucas's offer to help. She'd feared turning her problem over to her autocratic husband, afraid he'd want to run things, run her. Lucas had reached out to her in that moment, and her own misgivings had caused her to push him away.

She'd have to find a way to make it right. Just as soon as she knew her father would make it through this crisis.

When they'd finally located French in a homeless shelter, pneumonia had raged in his lungs and he was nearly unconscious with fever. Until last night, French had hovered on the edge of death, threatening to slip away at any moment. She could never have lived with herself if he had died and she hadn't been at his side.

Now the worst was past and French would soon be

moved back to the care home. Once she and Sherril and Stephen were certain he was stable, they'd all head home.

Enervated to the bone, Allie pushed herself to her feet and crossed to the window. The cloud-filled skies of an ugly gray January day did nothing to lift her spirits. Reno's backdrop of sere brown hillsides, so different from the familiar snowcapped Sierras east of Sacramento, only added to her alienation.

What was Lucas feeling right now? Anger? Hurt? She couldn't blame him—she'd kept secret French's ravaging debility, closed Lucas out of that circle of adults who shared the tragedy of a strong, vigorous man ruined by Alzheimer's. But he was her husband now. She should have told him. He deserved to share the griefs of her family as well as the joys.

She would tell him now, find a phone and call him. She needed his support as much as Sherril and Stephen needed the understanding of Pete and Anne. She would give anything right now to have him beside her, his hand gripping hers, shoring her up.

Lord, what a mess she'd made of things. She'd been too used to handling this pain herself. Sharing it with Lucas would have made the load lighter.

Striding back across the room, Allie grabbed up her purse and stepped out into the hall to find a pay phone. Her hand trembled as she dialed Lucas's number at TaylorMade.

Helen's cheerful voice answered, "TaylorMade."

"It's Allie. Is he there?"

"I'm afraid he's down in Modesto today. Another crisis. I can page him," Helen offered.

"No, don't." He had enough on his mind, she didn't

need to add to it. She'd be heading home soon; she could tell him then.

"Allie..." The sympathy in Helen's voice brought Allie to the edge of tears again. "I don't know what's going on between you two, but he looks terrible and he's acting worse." She continued in a no-nonsense tone, "He needs you, Allie. The sooner you can get back, the better."

Allie hung up, leaned against the wall, tried to order her thoughts. As she struggled with what to do, Sherril and Stephen exited the elevator and walked toward her.

"How is he?" Sherril asked, worry lining her face.

"Fine," Allie assured her. "Seems to be breathing a little easier this morning."

Stephen gave her shoulder a squeeze. "You should head back to the hotel, get some rest."

"Yes." Then clarity suddenly hit and Allie pushed away from the wall. "No. I need to get home. Would you two mind supervising getting Dad back to the care facility?"

Smiling, Sherril gave her a hug. "No problem. I keep forgetting you're a newlywed."

Was she? Sometimes it was hard to think of herself as married at all. But she loved Lucas, and right now, that was what mattered.

Ducking back into her father's room, she pressed a kiss on his weathered cheek. "Keep me updated, okay?" she said to her siblings as she left the room again.

Energized by her decision, Allie hurried to the elevator, then out to her car. At the hotel, she quickly packed, getting back on the road in less than thirty minutes.

Not even the scattered flakes of snow brushing the

Volvo's windshield discouraged her as she headed west on Interstate 80. She was going home, back to Lucas. Nothing short of a blizzard would hold her back. One way or another, she was going to explain about her father to Lucas. No more secrets.

Of course, as much as she might hope her willingness to reveal the truth about French's illness would encourage Lucas to do the same about his past, she knew that was unlikely to happen. She could only continue to love him, and pray that someday her devotion would peel away the layers Lucas wore around his heart. She would keep battering at his walls, beating down those doors he kept closed to her. Damned if she'd let him isolate himself from her love.

Her gaze fixed on the highway, Allie followed the curves of Interstate 80, her mind whirling with what she would say to Lucas. Somehow, she would convince her husband it was time to let her in.

Allie pulled out of the TaylorMade parking lot and headed for home. She'd barely stepped from the elevator before Helen informed her Lucas had gone home directly from the Modesto plant. Once the shock wore off that Lucas had put in less than a half day of work, Allie's worries kicked into overdrive. Was he sick? she demanded of Helen. Was something wrong with him?

Helen had given her a tolerant smile. "The only thing wrong is that you're not with him."

Standing before Helen's desk, she'd waffled—should she call Lucas to let him know she was on her way? Or would it be better if she surprised him?

She'd suspected Lucas didn't like surprises. But her thoughts were so scattered she wasn't sure she could speak to him coherently.

"Would you call him, please?" she asked Helen. "Let him know I'm coming?"

So now she covered the short distance from the office to home, doing her best not to speed down Douglas Boulevard. As she slowed to turn into the driveway, a nest of snakes seemed to take up residence in her stomach, writhing and tangling as she approached the house.

As much as she wanted to park at the front door and race up the stairs to be with him that much quicker, Allie forced herself to open the garage, pull the Volvo in and close the garage behind her. Lucas would have had to hear the hum of the automatic door opening, had to know it was her.

She left her purse, left her suitcase, left the key in the ignition. With shaking hands, she climbed from the car and strode purposefully for the interior door, her legs trembling in time with her hands.

He was waiting for her just inside. He stepped back as she came through the door and shut it carefully behind her. As she lifted her gaze to his, her heart stuttered at the sight of him.

He'd tossed off his jacket; it hung by one shoulder on a kitchen chair, its hem dragging on the floor. His shirt looked slept-in, his tie was knotted wrong. She guessed if he'd combed his hair that morning, he'd sent it into disorder long since by dragging his fingers through it.

But it was the beard shadow on his jaw that stunned her. Lucas's grooming had been impeccable for as long as she'd worked for him. Bad enough his clothes were awry; she couldn't fathom him going into the office with what looked like two-days' growth of beard.

The house, too, seemed in as much disarray as the man. Dirty dishes lay out on the kitchen counter and the wilted flowers on the breakfast table drooped from their vase.

"Hasn't Mrs. Vasquez been here?" Allie knew the housekeeper would never leave the house in this state.

He shook his head. "Gave her some time off."

Another puzzle piece that didn't fit. "Why?" she asked him.

His jaw worked, then he rasped out, "She asked me about you. I couldn't forget—" He bit the words off.

His gray eyes burned with a frightening intensity as he fixed his gaze on her. She tried to interpret what she saw there. Rage? Self-righteous arrogance? His chest heaved and his fingers curled at his sides as if he struggled between dark and light.

Just as she thought he would explode with anger, he took a step toward her. Smoothing the harsh lines of his face, a tenderness, a yearning flickered in his eyes. One step, another, then he flung his arms around her, holding her so tight at first he squeezed the breath from her lungs. Then he eased off and Allie couldn't hold back her laughter, her joy.

He buried his face in her hair. "You're back," he said hoarsely. "Thank God, you're back."

"Of course I am." She stroked along the tense muscles of his back, running her palms up and down.

"I was so afraid...." He pressed his lips to her throat. "When you called, I didn't want to talk. I thought I'd say the wrong thing, drive you away from me."

"You can't, Lucas. You won't ever drive me away." She leaned back, fixed her gaze with his. "I love you, Lucas."

Surely that was adoration in his soft gray eyes. For a heartbeat, she thought he would finally unlock the stronghold of his heart and tell her he loved her. But he remained silent until she had to put aside her hope.

It was time, she realized, time to tell him the truth. "Lucas, about my father—"

"You don't have to—"

"I do." Allie pushed herself to continue. "My father's illness…it's Alzheimer's. He's in the final stages. I should have told you a long time ago, but he's always been such a proud man, I knew he would hate anyone outside the family knowing."

"I thought we were a family," he said softly.

"We are, Lucas." She stroked his jaw, his beard rough against her fingertips. "I should have realized that before now."

His hand covered hers, pressed it against his face. "I haven't made it easy for you. It kills me that you've dealt with this alone when I should have shared the burden with you."

"We'll share it now, Lucas." A lightness filled her when she realized she would have Lucas's strength to buttress her own. "I promise I won't keep anything else from you."

"Everything I am now, everything I will be is yours." A troubled look clouded his intent gray gaze. "But my past…"

His past might be forever closed to her. But what did that matter when she had the man he was now? "We look forward, Lucas, from now on."

Quickly, she told him the rest of it, how her father's condition had deteriorated over the last several months, his near-fatal pneumonia that had kept her at his bedside for so long.

"The money I borrowed from you was for him," she told Lucas. "Even after moving him to a cheaper care home in Nevada, the costs ate up his pension, then my savings. I didn't know where else to turn. I couldn't burden my sister and brother.''

"Why didn't you tell me?'' he asked, then put a finger to her lips to forestall an answer. "You have as much stubborn pride as I do.''

"Then you forgive me?'' she asked, the feel of his finger against her mouth tantalizing.

"I'm the one who should ask forgiveness, for all I've put you through.'' He leaned down to claim her lips with his. His kiss was rough with passion and pent-up need. She responded instantly, heat burning along her veins.

His tongue thrust inside, again and again, teasing hers, dueling, then pulling back. She curved her hand around the back of his head, wanting to hold him there, bring him even closer. His coarse beard abraded her face, an intimate reminder of his agony without her.

He kissed along her jaw, grazed her earlobe with his teeth. "Is it safe?'' he whispered. "Safe for the baby if we make love?''

"Yes,'' she murmured in response, the word broken when the tip of his tongue traced the shell of her ear. "The doctor said we can't hurt the baby.''

He bent then, lifting her in his arms, at the same time covering her mouth with his again. One long, breath-stealing kiss, then he carried her to the stairs. Three steps then another kiss, all the way to the top, until she thought she would die with wanting him.

He headed for his own room, nudging the door open then kicking it shut again. As he set her down beside the neatly made bed, his hands cradled her denim-covered hips. Edging up her thick cotton sweater, he splayed his hands around her belly, his eyes closing.

"Our child," he whispered.

"Yes," she murmured back to him. "You're going to be a father."

"But can I—" He dipped his head and shadows concealed his features. The plantation shutters in his room still lay closed against the sun and the dim light wasn't sufficient to reveal his secrets. Allie could only guess by the tension in his shoulders and arms the turmoil inside him.

She realized that for her, making love would bring them closer, create the intimacy she craved. But for him, expressing himself sexually made it easy to remain behind his barriers.

She wanted him nonetheless.

Kicking off her sneakers, she unbuttoned her jeans and drew down the zipper. Following her lead, he hooked his fingers in the waistband of her jeans and pulled them down and off. He stripped off her sweater in one swift move, then straightened, his hands going to his tie.

With a smile, Allie grabbed the dangling silk and tugged him toward her. "Let me."

Reaching up, she unthreaded the knot on the tie and slid it slowly from around his neck. Trailing her fingers up his chest, she slipped the top button of his shirt free, then continued with the others, her thumbs parting the opening as she went. When she reached the waistband of his slacks, she tugged at the shirt, releasing it bit by bit before undoing the last two buttons.

As he shrugged free of the shirt, Lucas's hands closed on her shoulders, tightening when she unhooked his slacks. She lowered the zipper as slowly as she could, while Lucas's breathing throbbed in time to her own state of arousal. When his slacks finally fell from his hips and he stepped clear of them, Allie pressed against him, sending a long, low groan vibrating through him. Exultation burst within her at her power to excite him. If she couldn't bring his heart to love, at least she could give him this exquisite pleasure.

Lucas skimmed his briefs from his hips and let them fall to the floor. He pulled her against him, his hard length hot against her skin. She pressed her lips against his chest, the soft hair there brushing against her cheeks. She found his male nipples, running her tongue around one, then the other. As she laved them they stiffened to tight peaks and Lucas's breathing grew even harsher.

She ached to give him so much pleasure it would bind him to her in a way she couldn't hope to do with love. He understood the physical, the sexual; let it be her link to him.

His eyes nearly black with desire, he whispered hoarsely, "I want inside you."

"Please," she whispered back.

Chapter Fifteen

The intensity, the depth of his passion stunned Lucas. Even as his body demanded he take Allie and take her quickly, conflicting, incomprehensible emotions screamed at him to back away.

He let his body take over, stripping her bra and panties from her, jerking back the covers on the bed he hadn't slept in for a week. When he pressed her back against the pillow she gasped, no doubt at the chill of the sheets. He quickly covered her body with his, half-afraid the conflagration inside him would scorch them both.

He parted her legs with an impatient hand, ready to plunge inside her. "You're sure this won't hurt the baby?"

She didn't speak, just shook her head, lifted her hips to welcome him. The fetters of his logical mind shattered as he thrust inside her. He watched her eyes drift shut as she tightened around him, an exquisite sensation. She moaned, a long, low sound, and wrapped her legs around his hips.

Lord, he felt seventeen again and just as uncontrollable. If he didn't take a breath, muster some restraint, he'd go over the edge in a heartbeat.

Resisting the urgency to pound into her, he thrust slowly, deeply, keeping his face close to hers so he could watch her every response. A vivid flush colored her cheeks and her half-lidded eyes seemed lost in pleasure. Her nipples rubbed against his chest, the contact sending him on a path to madness.

As much as he wanted to see every moment of pleasure in her face, he gave in to the temptation to taste her lips, the sweetness of her mouth. Dipping his tongue past her lips, he stroked in imitation of his thrusting between her legs, a slow, mesmerizing pleasure. For the first time, he was glad he was forty, glad he could maintain the control that had eluded him as a younger man.

With her first moments of climax, her head pressed back into the pillow, fingernails digging into his sides as her legs locked at the small of his back. So close to the edge himself, he gritted his teeth against the oncoming wave, drawing out her climax as long as he could. Then the pressure of her muscles clenching around him heightened the sensations beyond what even he could resist and he let himself tumble into paradise with her.

His release was so intense, the world faded from his awareness, leaving him only the woman in his arms, the welcoming heat of her. He rasped out her name, clutched her so tight he was certain he was hurting her. Deep inside him, a voice cried out, shouting words he'd never dared to speak. Scrambling for a scrap of lucidity, he pushed back the pronouncement, burying his face in her throat to silence himself.

In the aftermath of pleasure, every muscle in his body warmed and relaxed. Not wanting to crush her with his weight, he slipped from her, gathering her in his arms as he lay beside her. The words he'd kept inside still rang in his ears and it frightened him a little that he'd nearly spoken them aloud.

She turned in his arms, facing him. Her eyes fluttered open and she smiled at him, her fingers tracing a path along his jaw, to his ear, along his throat. Her dazed, sated expression filled him with a fierce male pride.

She sighed, snuggled closer. "That was utterly divine."

He pressed a kiss to her forehead, her skin satiny against his lips. "Welcome home."

When he drew back, he could see Allie's devotion in her eyes. She repeated the words she'd said earlier. "I'll always come back home. I love you, Lucas."

He wanted to believe. A part of him even wanted to utter the same words back, even if they weren't in his heart.

She gazed at him, and he could see the expectant hope in her eyes. Not wanting to hurt her, knowing he couldn't help but cause her pain anyway, he remained silent. When hope dimmed in her face, she shut her eyes, edged even closer to him as if seeking the comfort his heart couldn't provide.

A bitterness settled in his chest that someone as sweet as Allie had saddled herself with him. He had nothing to give her, at least nothing to satisfy her yearning. He had only his body to offer and the sensuality between them.

As her legs tangled with his, he responded instantly, ready to pleasure her as before. She pressed against him, her hand at his hip to pull him closer, signaling to him that her desire matched his own.

Shifting to cover her body, he devoured her mouth with a kiss, drank in her sweetness. A trace of unease lingered inside him but he pushed it aside. She wanted him, he wanted her; right now that was all that mattered. If he couldn't bind her to him with love, he would do it with passion.

Surely that would be enough.

The day faded into night and Allie thought she would die of happiness. They came up for air long enough for a hurried dinner before returning to his bedroom to make love for what seemed the hundredth time. Then they showered in his lavish master bathroom and she sat on the edge of the tub, huddled in his terry robe, watching him shave, fascinated by the stark white towel hanging low on his hips.

Now he slept beside her in his bed, smelling clean and fresh from his shower. Sprawled on his stomach with his arms flung up, he had his face turned toward her, and the tension in his body was finally gone.

In the dim moonlight filtering in through the blinds, her gaze roamed over his face. She took in each beloved feature, imagined that high brow and stubborn chin on a son or daughter of his. She could see herself so clearly cradling Lucas's infant in her arms, nursing him or her as Lucas looked on.

Their child would be loved, respected, always cared for; she would make certain of that. Lucas still might think he didn't know how to love, but he'd demonstrated to Allie he could make a child feel cherished.

She need only remember his kindness toward her nephew Danny, the easy way he had with the children at the Christmas party.

Lucas's complexity, the layers of mystery surrounding him only made Allie love him more. He might never say the words she ached to hear from him, but that had begun to matter less and less. His actions spoke louder than any words. In that moment, she felt treasured.

Needing to touch him, Allie trailed her fingers across his back, down his spine, then up again over the rough scar spanning most of the right side of his back. In the time they'd been together, he hadn't yet told her where he'd gotten the scar. She wondered if he'd ever trust her enough to reveal that part of his past.

Spreading her hand, she stroked the uneven skin, wishing again she could smooth it, remove the memories that no doubt came with it. As broad as the mark was, and from its appearance, she guessed he'd been burned, and burned badly. Had he been an adult when it happened? Or, God help him, had he only been a child?

He must have sensed her touch in his sleep, because he stirred, his hands flexing above the pillow. But he didn't wake, just twisted under the covers as if trying to move away from some peril.

"Fire!" he blurted in his sleep, writhing under Allie's hand. "Too hot...Mom!"

Afraid she was adding to his nightmare with her touch, Allie broke the contact. But he remained ensnared in the dream images, fingers digging into the sheet as his breathing quickened.

"No!" He roared the single word, terror in the sound. "I can't...I can't... *Mom!*"

Frightened, near tears, Allie sat up, slapped on the bedside light. She grabbed Lucas's shoulder and shook him, shouting his name.

He turned his face away. The tendons in his hands stood out in sharp relief as his fingers clawed the sheet. "No, no, no…" he moaned, then screamed, as if caught by an agonizing pain.

Frantic now, Allie gripped his shoulder with two hands, leaned close to his ear. "Lucas! Wake up!"

One gasping breath and he shoved himself bolt upright, scrambling back from her in the bed. She knew his gray eyes, wide with remembered terror, didn't yet see her as he dragged in breath after breath. A shudder passed through his body as he stared blankly, then abruptly he came fully awake.

"Allie," he whispered, passing a hand over his face. He looked around him as if trying to work out where he was. "What…?"

"A dream. A nightmare," she answered. "I touched your scar. It must have set you off."

She tried to interpret the emotions flickering in his face—a trace of shame, embarrassment. Then he surprised her by sliding closer to her, cupping her cheek. "Thank you. For waking me."

He kissed her, pressing his lips lightly to hers. Gathering her into his arms, he leaned back against the headboard. When she shivered against the chill on her bare skin, he tugged the covers up over them both.

He didn't ask her to turn out the light and she made no move to do so. He just sat beside her, a pensive expression on his face as he ran his fingers up and down her arm.

Allie tipped her head up to him. "How did it happen, Lucas?" she asked in a quiet voice.

He didn't answer right away, just gazed out at the shadowy room. "A fire," he said finally.

"When? How long ago?"

He sighed, shutting his eyes. "Nearly thirty years."

When he was ten. Allie's heart lurched. "What happened?"

A familiar tension tightened his jaw and his light caresses ceased. "An apartment fire." She felt the pressure of each individual fingertip on her arm. "I didn't get out quick enough."

The trace of self-blame in his statement alarmed her. "It wasn't your fault was it?" She pulled away slightly to look up at him. "You didn't start the fire?"

She saw surprise in his face as he met her gaze. "No. It was a wiring short."

Relief washed over her. The fire must have been horrifying enough; if he still carried the guilt of being responsible for it, a man as intense as Lucas might never forgive himself. "What a terrible thing for a child to go through."

"If I could have put it out...if I could have..." Shaking his head, he seemed to throw off the old memories. Then he leaned in to kiss her as his fingers resumed their caresses on her arm. "Allie," he murmured. "You make me crazy."

Drawing her down to the bed, he covered her body with his. He entered her so swiftly, it stole her breath, slammed her heart into overdrive. His deep, thrusting kisses, his fingers teasing her nipples quickly drove her to climax.

Later, with the light off again and his body spooned against hers, Allie marveled at how well he'd learned the secrets of her body. But as she drifted off to sleep, she couldn't quite shake the feeling that as much as he'd revealed to her that night, he still hid behind one last barrier. Somehow, she had to find a way to break through it.

After that long, passionate day and night, Allie felt her marriage to Lucas had begun anew. His tender solicitude at work and at home delighted her, made her feel cherished and protected. He took pains to treat her kindly, tempering his usual abrupt, arrogant demands, his tone with her gentler, more caring.

He touched her often, even at work, his fingers lingering on her shoulder or his hand taking hers when they walked together to a meeting. If he felt awkward with his displays of affection in front of his staff, he never showed it. He seemed determined to declare to the world his connection to her, his claim on her.

His near-obsessiveness about their baby-to-be Allie put down to the anxiety of a first-time father. Although at first he'd seemed hesitant to talk about her pregnancy, the intimate turn to their relationship broke the logjam. He began peppering her with questions—about her due date, her diet, whether she planned to breast-feed. That last question shocked her a bit until she discovered a well-thumbed copy of a baby book in his nightstand drawer.

When he demanded to know her doctor's name, insisted she switch from her familiar ob-gyn to a high-priced big-name physician, she put her foot down. He didn't take her refusal well until he accompanied her to her next appointment, saw the attentiveness of the doctor and her nurse practitioner. He'd grudgingly agreed she'd made a good choice.

Sixteen weeks along, Allie was torn between delight at his interest and exasperation at his unrelenting inquiry. As he stood at her side in the doctor's examination room for her first ultrasound, he never let up his third degree of Dr. Singh.

Gripping Allie's hand, he confronted the unflappable obstetrician as if she were a corporate enemy. "She's still sick to her stomach. Shouldn't that have stopped by now?"

Prone on the examination table, Allie gave the doctor an apologetic smile. "Pregnancies don't all go by the book, Lucas."

"And what about weight gain?" Lucas asked. "She's only put on three pounds. It should have been four or five by now."

"Lucas," Allie said, then sucked in a breath as Dr. Singh squeezed ice-cold conductive gel on her belly. "I'm just as happy not to gain too much."

"Even still—"

"Take a look at your baby, Mr. Taylor," Dr. Singh said, pushing the ultrasound machine toward him to give him a better view. She moved the paddle on Allie's belly until the image cleared.

His mouth open to grill Dr. Singh further, he stilled, absolutely thunderstruck at his first view of the screen. Keeping his grip on Allie's hand, he moved closer to the machine. As Dr. Singh pointed out the head, the face, the tiny hands and feet of the sixteen-week-old fetus, Lucas listened, obviously entranced. The longing in his face as he gazed at that fuzzy, ill-formed image melted Allie's heart.

"He's ours, isn't he?" he asked, wonder in his voice.

"Can't be sure it's a boy yet," Dr. Singh said. "But yes, he or she is all yours."

Lucas swallowed convulsively as he seemed to absorb the reality of their baby. He turned to Allie, the awe still in his face, silencing him.

As they drove back to TaylorMade headquarters in a midmorning February drizzle, his silence lingered. Even when they reached the fifth floor and stepped from the elevator, he seemed in a daze as he wandered toward his office.

"Should we do the rundown now, Lucas?" Allie asked, reaching for her laptop.

"What?" He turned toward her, his shell-shocked expression nearly comical.

"Your appointments for the week," Allie said, reminding him of their morning routine. She brandished her computer.

"Yes, right." Opening his office door, he stepped aside to let her go in first.

She sat in her usual spot opposite his desk, setting her computer on her lap. Bringing up the scheduling program, she read off each day's commitments. She could see from his face that little of what she told him registered. She'd probably have to tell him the details again before the day was out.

When his phone rang, he looked at it in surprise as if not quite sure what to do. Then he finally shook off his haze and snatched up the receiver. "Taylor," he snapped out.

After listening a moment, he glanced up at her, holding up a finger to let her know he needed to take the call. When she made a move to rise, he motioned her back down. Allie busied herself with rechecking her entries to be sure she'd forgotten nothing.

His gaze strayed to her often as he spoke, as if to constantly assure himself she was still there. Although it touched her that she had become so important in his life, for his sake, she wished he would learn to trust that she would never leave him.

She felt the faintest of fluttering and reflexively pressed a hand to her belly. His sharp eyes caught the gesture, narrowing in concern. She smiled to calm him, lightly rubbing her belly and wondering if what she felt had been the baby moving or something as mundane as gas. She had another four weeks until the five-month mark, when Dr. Singh said she would most likely feel movement.

Lucas finally set down the phone. "Sorry. The Modesto plant had another breakdown. Where are we?"

Curving her arms around her swelling belly to reach her laptop's keyboard, Allie hit a key to clear the screensaver. "Let's see, we were…" By mistake, she exited the scheduling program. She clicked the icon again, laughing. "I can't quite get used to the extra baggage."

He smiled, the rare sight melting her clear to her toes. "My mother once told me I kept her awake nights when she was pregnant with me."

Allie's breath caught in her throat. It was the first time he'd mentioned his mother without prompting, without the bleakness in his voice, in his eyes. Allie wanted to take the moment to ask him a million questions about her but she knew she didn't dare. Not yet.

She paged through the scheduling display, looking for where they'd left off. "Actually, we were just about done. You have that meeting next week with the New Jersey contingent. Friday afternoon."

"Good," he said, rising to his feet. He rounded the desk, plucked the computer from her lap. Taking her hands, he tugged her to her feet, then pulled her close.

He cupped her bottom, pressing her to him. "No matter how often we make love, I can't seem to get enough."

Sensation tingled down her spine, settled between her legs in a honeyed warmth. Her arms around him, she felt his heat through the crisp dress shirt. "Somehow your loving always makes me want more," she murmured against his chest.

His breathing took on a ragged edge. "You are too damn tempting. If I wasn't afraid we'd be putting on a show for the staff, I'd take you right here."

Moving her lips against his shirt, she felt his nipple peak. "The door is shut."

He groaned. "But the windows aren't."

She followed his pointed look out the wall of windows overlooking the TaylorMade campus. Staff crisscrossed the verdant green lawn below as they headed to or returned from the cafeteria for morning break.

"They're five stories down, Lucas. They'd never see us on the floor."

He stared down at her, his gaze burning her. Then he threw back his head and laughed, an incredible sound of joy and release. He pinned her with his gaze again, caught her chin in his hand. "You are incorrigible."

He kissed her, sizzling her clear to her toes, then drew back again, looking down at her. "Your body's changing."

"Expanding is more like it." She sighed, delight and chagrin mixing in equal measure over the alterations. "Everything seems to be swelling up."

He brought his hand up to cup her now very full breast. "I can't say I mind." His thumb stroked the tip, driving a moan from her.

"That floor is looking mighty good, Mr. Taylor," she whispered.

He chuckled, the sound low and sensual. "Let me lock the door."

He'd shifted, taken a step toward the door when a knock sounded. "Yes?" he called out, his tone clipped and impatient.

"I'm sorry, Mr. Taylor." Helen's voice sifted through the barrier, hesitant. "I need to speak to Allie."

Allie couldn't help it, she burst into giggles. Lucas scowled at her, but she knew his heart wasn't in the dark gesture. Opening the door, he kept it between him and Helen, no doubt to hide the way their sexual play had affected his body.

If Helen wondered at Allie's laughter, she had the discretion to suppress her curiosity. As Allie passed Lucas, he cocked a brow at her. "Lunch at home?" he asked. She winked at him in response, then followed Helen from the office.

"Sorry to disrupt your meeting," the older woman said with a straight face. "I can't find those blank CD-ROM disks marketing needs for their presentation. Randy said you knew where they were."

"I know where I left them," Allie said, heading for the supply room.

When she stepped inside the small, cluttered room, Helen behind her, Allie scanned the jam-packed shelves. She backed up as far as she could, her backside coming up against a filing cabinet as she peered at the top shelf.

"When the order arrived, I shoved them up top. Can't quite see if they're still there." Allie turned to

Helen. "Can you hand me that stepladder behind the door?"

Helen wrangled the stepladder out, pushed it open on the floor in front of the shelves. "Maybe I ought to go up," she suggested.

"Helen, I'm only four months pregnant. I can still climb a ladder."

Using the shelves to steady her, she ascended the three broad steps of the ladder until her chin was level with the top shelf. "There they are. Back behind the manila folders."

Not foolish enough to try and lift the heavy box of folders, she shifted enough items on the shelf until she could shove the folders aside. Then she leaned forward, fingertips reaching for the package of CD-ROM disks.

"What the hell are you doing!" Lucas's voice roared from the doorway.

Startled, Allie jumped, gripping the shelf edge to regain her equilibrium. But the inexorable changes in her body had altered her center of balance. For a moment, she felt disoriented, banging her ankle on the stepladder's railing as she tried to compensate. Suddenly, she felt herself falling and panic flooded her.

Lucas caught her before she reached the floor, but couldn't save her from whacking her head on the edge of the filing cabinet. Dazed, she brought a shaky hand up to feel her head as Lucas gripped her tightly. "Are you all right? Damn it, Allie, are you okay?"

She stroked the tender back of her head, grateful there was no blood. "I'm fine, Lucas." The words seemed to come out at a whisper; she cleared her throat and said more loudly. "Put me down. I'm fine."

But he didn't, carrying her from the supply room and

up the corridor to his office. "Call an ambulance," he barked at Helen. "Someone get me a blanket."

In his office, he set her gently in his chair and quickly probed her head. "Ow!" Allie cried, pushing his hands away. She felt centered again, back to normal. "Lucas, it's just a little bump. I don't need an ambulance, for heaven's sake."

The tremors in his hands resting on her shoulders, the terror in his face shocked her. "What about the baby?" he rasped out.

Her first thought was to make light of the incident, to laugh it off. But she had only to see the real fear in his eyes to know he was deadly serious.

She covered his hands with her own. "The baby's fine, Lucas. We're both fine. A little bump on the head won't hurt her." She took his hand, brought it to her lips. "Or him."

He seemed only marginally comforted. "Are you sure?"

Rubbing her cheek against the back of his hand, she tried to assure him with the contact. "As sure as I can be." She tipped her head back, looked up at him. "Babies are tough. And you caught me in time."

"But I couldn't keep you from hitting your head."

"You can't protect me from every danger."

Despite the truth in them, her words did nothing to soothe him. His jaw working, he fixed his sharp gaze on her. "I want you to see your doctor."

She could do that much for him. Looking past him, Allie saw Helen waiting in the doorway. "No ambulance, Helen. But could you call Dr. Singh for me, set up an appointment for this afternoon? The number's in my Rolodex."

When Helen had gone, Lucas sank to one knee and

drew her into his arms. She held him, feeling his trembling slowly ease as she stroked his back. "I love you, Lucas," she whispered in his ear, wanting to soothe with love in a way her touch couldn't always accomplish.

He sighed, relief in the sound. After a moment, he withdrew, rising to his feet. When Helen returned to tell Allie Dr. Singh had squeezed her in at one-thirty, Lucas seemed to have stepped back behind his barriers. Giving Helen a brusque nod, he informed Allie he'd be back at one-fifteen to drive her to the appointment, then strode from the room, muttering something about R and D.

No more tenderness, no more mention of a lunchtime rendezvous. Allie stared after him, astounded at his quicksilver change.

Helen put a sympathetic hand on Allie's shoulder. "Not an easy man to love, I guess."

Allie just shook her head, winced at the pounding that had commenced there. Squeezing her eyes shut, she asked Helen, "Would you mind getting my purse? I need something for my head."

Helen brought her purse and a small paper cup of water. As Allie shook the painkillers into her palm, she caught sight of Lucas moving along the pathway below, heading for the building housing Research and Development. Just as he reached the front door, his steps slowed and he propped his shoulder against the thick glass as if he desperately needed the support.

As she watched, he dropped his head, stood motionless that way for several long moments. When staff members exited beside him, he seemed oblivious to their curious looks, seemed caught in his own hell.

Allie's heart ached seeing him that way. She wished

she could send her love across that space to him, to reassure him.

He looked up then, his gaze seeking her out although he couldn't see her through the reflective glass of his office window. As if somehow knowing she watched and gathering strength from that knowledge, he pushed off from the glass, shoulders straight again. Then he slipped inside the building, gone from her sight.

Chapter Sixteen

Allie should have known Dr. Singh's assurances wouldn't satisfy Lucas. Although Allie showed no signs of concussion, and the doctor insisted both baby and mother were fine, Lucas's stony silence told Allie he wasn't buying any of it. Then as he drove her home—not back to the office as she'd requested, but home—she could see from the tension in his jaw a battle was brewing.

When they stepped inside the house, he helped her off with her jacket with angry, jerky movements, not even acknowledging Mrs. Vasquez in the kitchen. Allie met the housekeeper's gaze with an apologetic smile.

Dropping the jacket on a kitchen chair, he rounded on Allie. "You have to quit your job," Lucas stated flatly. "Now."

At Lucas's lordly demand, Mrs. Vasquez's eyes widened, then she dipped her head back to her dinner prep-

arations. Irritation growing inside her, Allie counted to
ten. Then in as rational a tone as she could muster, she
said, "Lucas, I think you're overreacting—"

"The hell I am!"

Startled, Mrs. Vasquez dropped the kitchen knife she
was using; it skittered across the floor. "Excuse me,"
she said, her face flaming. "Maybe I should—"

"Stay," Allie said, putting up a hand to stop the
housekeeper. "Mr. Taylor and I will go upstairs."

Turning on her heel, she stomped over to the stairs,
not bothering to look back to see if he followed. She
heard his heavy tread behind her, waited for him to
catch up when she reached the second-floor landing.
He pushed open his bedroom door, let her go in first.

Once he'd shut the door again, she faced him, arms
crossed over her middle. "I'm not quitting my job."

"Then I'm firing you."

She gaped at him. "You can't be serious."

"I am," he said coldly. "If you won't quit, I'll fire
you. One way or another, you're leaving your job."

It took Allie a moment to gather her wits in the face
of his unreasonable stance. She took a step toward him.
"You have no grounds to fire me."

"It's a hazardous work environment."

She shook her head in disbelief. "Lucas, you know as
well as I do, there's nothing hazardous at TaylorMade.
Not to mention the discrimination laws you'd violate ter-
minating me."

"I don't care." His jaw worked. "We can't take the
chance."

Suddenly Allie realized it wasn't Lucas's arrogance
that drove him to make such an outrageous demand.
His very real fear for the baby had prompted him to

lash out, to act in the only way he knew, as inappropriate as it was.

Allie couldn't allow him to control her that way, but she'd have to tread cautiously. "I can't live the next six months in a protective bubble."

"It would be better for the baby if you were home."

"I'm as likely to have an accident here as at the office." She saw his eyes widen and spoke quickly to head off an even more restrictive edict. "But I won't. I'll be fine, here or at TaylorMade."

His hands opened and closed, his frustration evident in the repetitive, unconscious motion. "I'm only trying to keep you safe."

She closed the distance between them, ran her hands along his arms. "I know. And I know you're doing your best. But sometimes life jumps up with surprises."

His expression turned bleak, reminding her that he knew plenty about surprises—that long-ago fire, the death of his mother.

Allie wrapped her arms around him, pressed her cheek to his chest. His heart thudded in comforting rhythm. "I promise you," she said, "I'll stay off ladders. I won't lift anything heavier than my laptop. I'll be as careful as I can possibly be."

He let out a long gust of air. "I can't stand the thought of something happening to you or the baby." The words seemed dragged out of him, as if by speaking them, he introduced the possibility of calamity.

"I feel the same way…about you, about the baby." She leaned back slightly to look at him. "But if I'm at work, you can watch me like a hawk. Keep me out of trouble."

The sense of that sank in and to Allie's relief and

delight, Lucas smiled. "I may have to drag you every-where with me. Every meeting, every plant visit."

The light in his eyes sent joy arrowing through her. "I'd like nothing better."

He dipped his head, covering her mouth with his, diving in with his tongue. Her body warmed immedi-ately, sensation exploding from her center.

"Why can't I get enough of you?" he murmured, the words feathering on her cheek.

Because you love me, she wanted to say. *I can see it in your eyes, why won't you say it aloud?* For all the times she'd told herself his returning her love didn't matter, she couldn't get past the ache inside that his silence caused her.

She pushed aside the doubts, the pain, letting him unzip her skirt, push off her sweater. He left her long enough to lock the door, then finished undressing her before stripping off his own clothes. Urging her to the bed, he jerked back the covers, then pulled her down with him.

Lying on his back, he positioned her over his hips. She straddled him, the hard length of his arousal press-ing into her.

When she tried to lie down, he circled her waist with his hands, held her in place. "I want to watch you," he rasped out. Lifting her, he groaned as he slid inside her, his eyes shutting a moment before he fixed his gaze on her again.

Stroking up with his hands, he spread his palms over her breasts, teasing the tips until they hardened. "I like how they're fuller, bigger." He leaned up high enough to take an exquisitely sensitive nipple in his mouth, tormenting it with the tip of his tongue.

Allie threw back her head and moved her hips in a

familiar rhythm. He lay back again, watching her every move, one hand dropping to her tender nub while the other continued to stroke her breast.

His eyes burned like molten silver. "Come apart for me, Allie." His inexorable demand shot straight through her. "Let me see you climax."

She couldn't deny him. The pressure of his thumb between her legs, the length of him pushing inside her sent pleasure coursing through her. She felt impossibly hot, excruciatingly sensitized, her love for him bursting out and taking the ecstasy to an unbearable level.

She spiraled out of control, the world disappearing from her for a heartbeat, only Lucas's body and his triumphant voice real to her in that moment. Just as she descended, he shocked her into another peak, his clever fingers driving her on. When he finally came himself, his climax pushed her over the edge a third time, reverberating through her.

She sank beside him, too enervated to hold herself up any longer. He pulled her into his protective embrace, cradling her head against his shoulder. His fingers wove into her hair, the gentle caresses easing her back to reality.

"Tell me," he whispered, his fingers combing through her hair.

She couldn't possibly deny him. "I love you, Lucas."

Why had he asked her? When he couldn't respond in kind, when no matter how he tried, those same feelings eluded him. Lucas knew he cared deeply for Allie; she meant the world to him. Losing her would devastate him. But when he probed inside himself, searching for the same devotion she gave him so freely, he came up empty. It simply didn't seem within his capacity to love her.

A coldness stole inside him, chilling him clear to the bone. His inability to love Carol hadn't bothered him overmuch in the four years he'd been married to her. He'd never lied to her, never made her think he felt something he didn't. When she finally confronted him and told him she could no longer live with him as his wife without having her love reciprocated, he'd given Carol her freedom with few regrets and not a small amount of relief.

But, good God, what if Allie reached the same conclusion? What if the day came when her heart could no longer bear the loneliness of unreturned love? He couldn't possibly let her go, couldn't comprehend his life without her.

Would their baby be enough to tie her to him? As incredible a mother as Allie would be, their child would surely adore her. Would that bond be enough for Allie to overcome the grief of a husband who couldn't love her back?

"Lucas," she murmured, her gaze troubled.

A fist constricted inside him as his fears ran amok. For an instant, the terror of losing her, although entirely in his own mind, closed in on him, blacked out his world.

With an effort, he refocused his awareness on Allie. "Yes?"

She frowned a little at his brusque tone. "Is something the matter? Because you're gripping me so tight I can barely breathe."

He immediately relaxed, saw with chagrin the marks his fingers had left on her arm. "Sorry."

She gazed up at him awhile longer, then snuggled

against him, her face buried in his shoulder. "Too late to go back to work, I suppose." He could hear the teasing smile in her voice.

"Mrs. Vasquez should be gone soon. We could go downstairs and see what she left us for dinner."

"I'm not hungry yet." She shifted, sliding her body on top of his. "Not for food anyway."

Remarkably, his response to her was as strong as the first time. He turned, reversing their positions, running lips and tongue over every sensitive inch of her body until she climaxed again. He could love her this way— strum her body to completion, tie her with chains of passion. It might be a pale substitute for real love, but it was the best he could do.

She couldn't, wouldn't leave him. She had to stay. Because he couldn't live without her.

By mid-March, when the baby's movements became certain, each flutter eagerly anticipated and enjoyed, Allie thought she'd finally accepted the limitations of her marriage. She'd told herself again and again Lucas's respect and caring were enough, that those feelings were powerful enough in their own right to be equivalent to love.

Her father had recovered from the pneumonia and although still frail, was reasonably healthy. Lucas now accompanied her regularly to the care home, joining her and her sister's and brother's families. His presence shored her up during the difficult visits, when her father didn't know her, when he lashed out at her angrily as if she were a stranger.

In the past, when she'd dealt with the heartbreak alone, when even her family's presence couldn't soothe the ache of slowly losing her father, she'd spent the drive home in tears. But having Lucas at her side changed everything, made the pain bearable. Now she rode home afterward with her hand in his, the contact giving her strength.

Surely that meant as much as his love. And she should be happy with what Lucas could give her rather than pine for what he could not. Or at least she told herself time and again, convincing herself she believed it.

She gave herself that silent lecture again as she sat before the vanity mirror in the bathroom she now shared with Lucas. Light filtering through the skylight above her softly dappled her skin with the pattern of the overhanging oak branches. Craning her neck up to look through the skylight, she saw the pale green of new leaves bursting into life.

The arrival of spring should lift her spirits, but a tightness seemed to have lodged inside her that she just couldn't shake. As ashamed as she felt at her inability to fully appreciate the blessings she did have, she returned over and over to the sense of loss at what she didn't possess. She felt like a fraud every time she looked into Lucas's eyes and told him she loved him. Because although she did indeed, although she prayed each day he would open his heart to her, she herself had begun to close up a part of herself inside.

Allie sighed as she finished applying her makeup. After telling Lucas the truth about her father, she thought she'd put aside all her secrets. But now one burned inside, threatening to fester. As much as she might want it to be so, she was discovering it wasn't enough to simply love him without hope of reciprocation. Greedy as she was, she wanted it all.

Caught up as she was in her musing, she didn't hear

him enter the bathroom. When he suddenly appeared behind her, his image in the mirror startled her. She gasped, guilt coloring her face.

"Hello," she said to his reflection. She picked up her lipstick with a shaky hand. "Give me one more minute and I'll be ready."

"No hurry. Party doesn't start for another twenty minutes." He bent to hook his arms loosely around her, his hands resting against her swollen belly. "How's he doing?"

"She's fine." Finished with the lipstick, she tucked it into her handbag. "Active today."

He waited, his expression intense in the mirror. When a flutter rippled across her belly, his eyes widened in reaction. "Was that it? Was that him?"

"It was her," she said, laughing. She shifted in her chair, rising to put her arms around him. Gazing up at him, she murmured, "I love you, Lucas."

His eyes shone as he smiled down at her. "Thank you," he said softly. "For loving me."

The little knot inside her squeezed tighter. Angry at herself, she dropped her gaze, slipped away from him. "We should go."

He grabbed for her hand before she could escape. "We can be late." Pulling her toward him, he kissed the corner of her mouth, her cheek, trailing his lips to her ear. "Come to bed with me," he whispered.

Even as temptation tugged at her to do exactly that, to enjoy the purity of their physical connection, the shut-down part of herself said no. "My sister will have a fit if I'm late for her birthday party."

Sherril wouldn't, but Allie swept that thought aside as they headed out to the car. On the way to *Cocina Caldera,* where the families were meeting for the party, she and Lucas discussed company business—the snail's pace of repairs at the Modesto plant, the search for someone to replace her during her maternity leave.

As they pulled into *Cocina Caldera*'s parking lot, Lucas reached across the front seat to take her hand. "I promise, no more work talk. It's a weekend, it's your sister's party. I plan to devote the rest of the afternoon and evening to you."

He brushed his lips against the back of her hand, then let her go. Inside the restaurant, the lunch crowd had already left and it was early yet for the dinner group. Teresa greeted them effusively, escorting them through the nearly empty restaurant to the room in back reserved for the party.

Sherril, Stephen and their families were already there. To Allie's surprise, Lucas's friend, John, was there, as well, at one end of the long table.

As Inez set out baskets of chips and bowls of salsa, her gaze often strayed to John and each time sparks flew between them.

Allie turned to Lucas. "How long has that been going on?"

Lucas smiled. "A week or so. John finally got up the nerve to ask her out."

Inez passed by John on the way to the kitchen, lingering to whisper in his ear and brush a kiss on his cheek.

Allie laughed. "Doesn't look like she needed much persuading."

Sherril approached and patted Allie's tummy. "How's my niece doing?"

They spent the next half hour chatting about pregnancy and babies, Stephen's wife Anne joining in the conversation. Then dinner arrived, an array of special dishes Teresa had concocted just for Sherril. After the hearty meal, Inez served cake and Sherril opened her gifts, exclaiming over each one while the restless children played tag around the table.

Afterward, when they were all too stuffed to move, the men and women gravitated to opposite ends of the table. Inez, eager to get off her feet, sat with Allie, Anne and Sherril, her fingers linked with John's across the table.

At one point Lucas's gaze locked with Allie's, his hungry look enough to make her blush. Sherril, too sharp-eyed to miss the exchange, laughed as she gave Allie's arm a gentle poke. "That man is absolutely besotted with you."

Allie just smiled, her eyes downcast. Anne sighed as she looked across the room at her own husband. "I remember those days. Stephen told me he loved me a dozen times a day. Now I'm lucky to hear it once or twice a week."

"But he still adores you," Sherril said. "Like Pete— even when he doesn't say the words aloud, I still see it in his eyes."

As Anne agreed, Allie sought out Lucas again at the other end of the table. He met her gaze, smiling as his eyes roved her face. She saw the incipient passion, his desire. But was there love?

Knowing the answer, she looked away, afraid her disappointment would show in her face. She tried to focus on Sherril's and Anne's description of their progenies' most recent antics, but the joy of the party had gone out of her. Now she just wanted to go home.

She gestured to Lucas, said her goodbyes to her family. Once in the Mercedes, tiredness weighted Allie down, although it was still early evening. Leaning back, she closed her eyes, for the moment wanting to shut out the world.

Flicking a glance over at Allie, seeing her shut eyes and the tired lines of her face, disquiet stirred within Lucas. As he started the engine and pulled away, he looked at her sidelong, willing her to open her eyes and smile at him. But she kept her eyes closed as they drove, her hands linked over their growing child.

He'd sensed something was brewing inside Allie for some time, despite the easy contentment into which their marriage had settled. He'd caught the sadness in her eyes, read the despair that sometimes stole into her face. Even as he held her close and tried to pretend everything was fine, he knew something lurked beneath the surface.

If he ignored his misgivings, thrust them aside as he had been doing, he could continue to believe in the solidity of their marriage. But he had only to look at Allie, see the loneliness, the sorrow she worked so hard to conceal, and he realized there was no profit in delaying the inevitable.

He swallowed against a dry throat, keeping his gaze fixed on the twilight falling around them. "Allie," he rasped out, "what's wrong?"

She opened her eyes, but didn't look at him. Just as well; he was terrified he would read the secrets in her eyes. Clutching the Mercedes' steering wheel like a lifeline, he could feel the tendons popping out in his hands in sharp relief.

The silence ticked away, tightening the anxiety in his gut. When she finally spoke, he could hardly hear the words. "Lucas, I'm so sorry."

For a moment the air seemed wrenched from his lungs, then he said carefully, ''For what, Allie?''

She drew in a hitching breath. ''I thought it would be enough. But it isn't.''

The answers screamed at him, adding to his terror. With the forced actions of an automaton, he moved his foot to the brake, slowing for the red light ahead. Then with a deliberate effort, he asked, ''What's not enough?'' Although he knew.

''Loving you,'' she said through tears, ''without you loving me.'' She struggled to take in another breath. ''You don't love me, do you?''

His heart slammed in his chest, loud as a klaxon. As he shifted his foot to the accelerator again, he wondered how he would ever be heard over the cacophony. ''What do you want, Allie? Do you want me to say the words?''

''You would to please me, wouldn't you? But you wouldn't mean it. Wouldn't feel it.''

Lie to her! Lie to her now! But as many times as he'd hidden the truth from her about his past, he could give her nothing less than honesty about this. ''I want to, Allie. But no, I don't know how.''

She sniffed, the sound of her heart breaking as audible as shattered glass. Everything inside Lucas had shut off except the mechanical—scan ahead for traffic, flip on the blinker to change lanes, ease the car over. Keeping the car in control suddenly seemed crucially important.

This is it, my final failure. He couldn't love her, the most precious, most important part of his life, essential to his very being and he couldn't give her the one small thing she begged for.

He had to ask the ultimate question, the one that

dangled between them like a razor-sharp knife. "Are you going to leave me?"

He took his eyes off the road long enough to hear her answer, compelled to see her face as she replied. For an instant she met his gaze, agony and love in her eyes all at once. Then she glanced away and horror filled her face.

"Lucas, look out!"

He snapped his head back to the road, absorbing the nightmare in a heartbeat. The fast-approaching intersection. The pickup truck speeding along the cross street too fast to stop at the red light. The Mercedes rolling past the limit line as if in slow motion. The truck looming larger, closer to the car's passenger side. The first explosion of sound as tons of steel collided.

And Allie's scream, bursting inside him like a fatal bullet, tearing at the chambers of his heart. Screaming his name at the top of her lungs, her frightened keening a plea to help her, to save her. In the blackness that momentarily closed in, Allie's voice mingled with a long-dead memory and he heard his mother calling his name, screaming for him.

She was trapped, she was burning, please God, he had to save her. Her voice went on and on, loud and terrifying, until it was choked by the thick black smoke that seared his lungs and filled his eyes. Ten years old again, he struggled to see through the oily blackness, fought to breathe as he crawled along the floor.

He caught her hand, pulled at her still body. She moaned as he dragged her over the floor, heaving every ounce of his slight body against her dead weight. Looking over his shoulder at the open door he'd thought he could do it, could save her. But then a ceiling joist broke from its mooring, painting his back with fire before striking his mother.

He couldn't remember the rest, must have lost consciousness. But when he came to outside the apartment in the arms of a fireman, he could still hear his mother's screams in his mind. They just went on and on in his head, his name shrilled over and over.

With a sudden jolt, the memories released him and he stared, stunned, at Allie in the car beside him. The pickup truck had shoved aside half the engine compartment of the Mercedes and flames licked greedily from under the hood. Allie struggled weakly with her door, her head cut and bleeding, her eyes bruised with fear.

She turned to him, reached for him. ''I can't get it open, can't get the door open.''

He grabbed her, remembered the seat belt, fumbled to release the clasp. ''I've got you, I've got you—''

A sharp crack sounded as the flames licked closer and Allie screamed again. For a moment, the past dug its claws into him again, and it was his mother's hand he held. The impossibility of saving her swamped him, overwhelmed him. Then he shook free and gathered Allie into his arms.

Afraid she might be injured, that he might hurt her, he moved her as gently as he could. But the fire had ignited inside the cabin of the Mercedes, running along the plastic dash, melting the collapsed airbags with its voracious heat. Shoving open his partially sprung door, he lifted her from the car and staggered across the roadway to the sidewalk.

Even as the ambulance and fire truck pulled up, the fire reached the gas tank, setting off a massive explosion. Lucas held Allie close to him, rocking her as he caught sight of the driver of the truck moving on unsteady feet to the sidewalk. The man, swaying as if drunk, stared at the disaster he'd caused.

Lucas raised his head, shouted over the noise, "I need help! Someone help me here! She's hurt!"

As the paramedics hurried over, Allie's eyes drifted open. "I'm fine, Lucas. I was just scared. But you saved me."

Tears burned his eyes as he held her close. "I love you, Allie. I love you. You can't leave me."

"I won't. No, Lucas." She reached out for him as the paramedics lifted her onto a gurney, clutched his hand. "I would never leave you, I just..." Her eyes widened, fixed on him. "Did you say you love me?"

He wouldn't surrender her hand, even as the paramedics rolled her toward the ambulance. "I did. It's not just words, Allie. It's the truth." Tears clogged his throat. "I love you."

He leaned close, whispering in her ear. "I think my heart is finally open for you. I feel it now. I love you."

Straightening, he saw her eyes brim with tears, her wide, jubilant smile declaring her joy. "I love you, Lucas."

He clung to her hand as he climbed into the ambulance with her, drawing strength from her even as he lent her his own. He could tell her all of it, was more than willing to reveal all the secrets of his past. Because she'd healed those wounds with her sweetness and love.

As the ambulance pulled away, fear still assailed him for Allie, for the baby. As sensitive as ever, she saw it in his face, soothed him with the touch of her hand. "We'll both be fine."

And he knew in that moment, looking into her wide

green eyes, she was right. Their child had had a hell of a ride, but their love had made their baby strong, had made him a survivor.

"I love you," she whispered again, her gaze expectant.

His heart spoke the words silently even as he said them out loud. "I love you, Allie Taylor. Forever."

Epilogue

Allie sat in the shade of the covered deck, her newborn son nestled in her arms, while Lucas stood by the backyard swing watching their brand-new five-year-old daughter fly in ever increasing arcs. Her head thrown back in exuberant joy, Tiffany squealed to her father, "Higher, Daddy, higher!"

Lucas obliged, pushing the swing harder, grinning as his daughter sailed past him. Tiffany had come a long way since she'd arrived, sullen and silent, at their home four months ago. Her birth father dead, her natural mother lost to drugs, the tough-as-nails little girl had been a challenge from day one. Especially as baby Nathan lingered in Allie's womb a week past his due date, stubbornly setting his own birth agenda.

But they'd seen a turnaround in the last month since they'd started adoption proceedings for Tiffany. Most of the credit went to Lucas, his insight into all the shadowy corridors of Tiffany's heart giving him a wisdom Allie would never possess. Allie loved Tiffany and told her so every day. But Lucas added to his powerful love an understanding Tiffany had responded to instantly.

Month-old Nathan stirred in Allie's arms, gave out an exploratory screech as he rooted for her breast. Feeling a little like the local dairy, Allie lifted her blouse with a sigh and helped Nathan latch on. As demanding as his father, Nathan seemed to glare at her as he sucked, a commentary on her slow response time. She could only laugh, a softness spreading inside her as she gazed down at those wide gray eyes.

The accident six months ago had proved to be a turning point in more ways than one. The shattering of Lucas's barriers, his avowal of love for her had been miracle enough. But a day or two later, Lucas told her about Tiffany. He'd been discussing the little girl with John the night of Sherril's birthday party. Once he knew for certain Allie and the baby had survived the accident unscathed, he began campaigning to add Tiffany to their family. Not that Allie had needed much convincing.

Lucas facing the demons of his past, exposing them to Allie, had been cathartic for them both. She'd wept for him as he related the horror of the fire, his failed attempt to save his mother.

Even though Lucas had finally told her everything, it was taking time to cleanse the last of that old guilt from his soul. Allie's love for him and his for her had gone a long way toward healing him. But they both knew that before his imagined sins could be completely forgiven, he had to learn to love one more person— himself.

The nightmares, at least, had vanished. And although he still put on his lordly, autocratic airs from time to time, it took only a sweet smile from his daughter or the weight of his son in his arms to turn him into mush.

His unrelenting passion for Allie hadn't changed. Although their lovemaking had become a bit awkward near the end of her pregnancy, it had lost none of its fire. Now she counted down the days until they could be intimate again.

As if reading her mind, Lucas met her gaze, heat in his gray eyes palpable even from across the yard. He said something to Tiffany, then headed for the deck, his focus on Allie never wavering. When he reached her side, he brushed a kiss across her lips, his fingers lingering on her cheek.

"Two more weeks, huh?" he asked, glancing down at Nathan still busy at her breast.

"Afraid so," she sighed. "But you'll be the first to know when systems are go."

Pulling up a chair, he sat beside her, his shoulder touching hers. "I love you, Allie."

She reached for his hand, lifting it to her lips. "And I love you, Lucas Taylor."

As the August sun sank toward a fiery sunset, they watched their daughter play and their son drift off to sleep. Silently Allie gave thanks—for Lucas, for their children, but most of all for the miraculous love that enveloped them all.

* * * * *

MONTANA MAVERICKS

One of Silhouette Special Edition's most popular series returns with three sensational stories filled with love, small-town gossip, reunited lovers, a little murder, hot nights and the best in romance:

HER MONTANA MAN
by Laurie Paige
(ISBN#: 0-373-24483-5)
Available August 2002

BIG SKY COWBOY
by Jennifer Mikels
(ISBN#: 0-373-24491-6)
Available September 2002

MONTANA LAWMAN
by Allison Leigh
(ISBN#: 0-373-24497-5)
Available October 2002

True love is the only way to beat the heat in Rumor, Montana....

Where love comes alive™

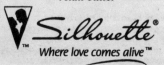

COMING NEXT MONTH

SSECNM0802